Philothée O'Neddy

The Enchanted Ring
A Romance of Chivalry

Translated and with an Introduction by
Brian Stableford

The Enchanted Ring

PHILOTHÉE O'NEDDY (1811-1875) was the pseudonym employed for his literary work by the poet baptized August-Marie Dondey, but who took to calling himself Théophile Dondey—from which name his anagrammatical pseudonym was derived—or Théophile Dondey de Santeny. Born in Paris in 1811, he joined Théophile Gautier's *petit cénacle* of young writers affiliated to the Romantic Movement, also known as Les Jeunes France, while still in his teens. He published a collection of poetry, *Feu et flamme* in 1933 and, in 1841, his most remarkable work of fiction, *L'histoire d'un anneau enchanté, roman de chevalerie.*

BRIAN STABLEFORD has been publishing fiction and non-fiction for fifty years. His fiction includes an eighteen-volume series of "tales of the biotech revolution" and a series of half a dozen metaphysical fantasies set in Paris in the 1840s, featuring Edgar Poe's Auguste Dupin. His most recent non-fiction projects are *New Atlantis: A Narrative History of British Scientific Romance* (Wildside Press, 2016) and *The Plurality of Imaginary Worlds: The Evolution of French* roman scientifique (Black Coat Press, 2016); in association with the latter he has translated approximately a hundred and fifty volumes of texts not previously available in English, similarly issued by Black Coat Press.

Contents

Introduction

"PHILOTHÉE O'NEDDY" was the pseudonym employed for his literary work by the poet baptized August-Marie Dondey, but who took to calling himself Théophile Dondey—from which name his anagrammatical pseudonym was derived—or Théophile Dondey de Santeny. Born in Paris in 1811, he joined Théophile Gautier's *petit cénacle* of young writers affiliated to the Romantic Movement, also known as Les Jeunes France, while still in his teens. He joined Gautier, Petrus Borel and Gérard de Nerval in the colorful and pugnacious group of supporters who attended the première of Victor Hugo's *Hernani* in February 1830, ready and eager to engage in fisticuffs with any claque appointed to disrupt the performance.

O'Neddy, one of the most flamboyant and outspoken members of the group, published a collection of poetry, *Feu et flamme* in 1933, optimistically announcing in its preliminary material the imminent publication of a novel, *Entre chien et loup*, and a "roman poétique," *La Lame et le fourreau*, but neither ever appeared. He also wrote a play in the 1830s, *Miranda*, which was never produced, and he toiled for many years on a long novel entitled *Sodome et Solime*, which he never finished, although two episodes appeared as *feuilletons* during a brief period in which he published a good deal of material in newspapers.

Unsuccessful at the time, *Feu et flamme* was belatedly recognized as an important precursor of the work of Charles Baudelaire; among other similarities, it employed the concept of *spleen* in the manner that Baudelaire was later to make famous. Most of O'Neddy's subsequent work only appeared in periodicals, if at all, until the publication by Georges Charpentier in 1877, two years after the poet's death, of a large collection of *Poésies posthumes*, followed a year later by an omnibus of his *Oeuvres en prose*.

O'Neddy's longest prose work, *Histoire d'un anneau enchanté, roman de chevalerie* (1841), here translated as *The Enchanted Ring: A Romance of Chivalry*, was the first of two novellas that he contrived to publish as *feuilletons* in *La Patrie*, a daily newspaper that published some of his theater criticism and poetry. The novella was reprinted in a cheap volume format in 1847 but that edition did not sell well and is now extremely rare. The other novella serialized in *La Patrie*, a feverish contemporary story of illicit amour, *Le Lazare de l'amour*, appeared there in 1843, but O'Neddy abandoned journalism soon thereafter, although much of the work he did for his own edification was carefully preserved by his sister, and thus remained available for posthumous publication. He never married, and lived with his sister and his mother; the latter died in 1861, after a long illness. In spite of his early political radicalism, Dondey worked throughout his adult life as a clerk in the Ministry of Finance, in order to support those two dependents, and was still doing so when the Siege of Paris began in 1870. Although in poor health, he survived the siege, the Commune and its brutal aftermath, but he retired in 1873.

Histoire d'un anneau enchanté, roman de chevalerie is a strange work, deliberately echoing some features of the enchanted world of twelfth and thirteenth-century French Romance, borrowing two key characters, Charlemagne and Archbishop Turpin from the *La Chanson de Roland* and dropping names from *Les Quatre fils Aymon* and *Renaud de Montauban*, but actually bearing little resemblance to those romances. It has some affiliations with the genre of French fantastic fiction descended from and developed in the wake of the *contes de fées* of the late seventeenth century, but it differs from them sharply in that, whereas they deliberately set their stories in a world devoid of Christianity, O'Neddy's story is replete with the imagery of that religion. It attributes some of its magic to Turpin, uses an archangel to kick-start the plot, and credits the most striking of its supernatural events to the direct intervention of God in answer to a prayer. Its heroine is compared to a fay, and certainly bears a strong resemblance to many heroines of *contes de fées* in terms of her exceptional beauty and virtue, but she only becomes an enchantress when she obtains a gift from God as a curious reward for good behavior, and her fate differs markedly from that of most heroines of the genre.

The longest of several authorial intrusions that the author makes into his text in order to comment on its narrative strategy offers an explanation of sorts of why the story does not follow the standard narrative trajectory of tales of enchantment, but the tongue-in-cheek sarcasm of those intrusions does not encourage the reader to take any of them too seriously—a double bluff, as O'Neddy certainly believed the critical remarks he made. He probably felt obliged to employ a careful measure of indirection in clarifying his own philosophy of procedure, given that *La Patrie,* where the feuilleton appeared, had an editorial policy some way to the right of most of the Parisian newspapers of the day, and he had to bear in mind that his readership probably included a considerable number of religious conservatives—whom he addresses directly, and a trifle combatively, in one or two of his intrusions.

The combination of circumstances affecting the novella's production and marketing undoubtedly helped to enhance the peculiarity of the story, but that does not detract at all from the fact that it is one of the most remarkable products of the French Romantic imagination. It is certainly eccentric—the Jeunes France were a defiantly and insistently eccentric gang—but all the more fascinating and intriguing for that. It has a fine flamboyance and an admirable zest, which maintain its readability very well into the twenty-first century. Although the proto-Baudelairean aspects of *Feu et flamme* have helped to maintain that volume's reputation at a higher level, *Histoire d'un anneau enchanté, roman de chevalerie* has an equal claim to be considered its author's masterpiece, and its translation is long overdue.

✳

The translation was made from the electronic version of the 1878 George Charpentier edition of *Oeuvres en prose* reproduced on the Bibliothèque National's *gallica* web-site. That version supplements the novella with a plaintive poetic epilogue that appeared in *La Patrie* in 1842, which I have similarly added to the translated text, in a literal translation that makes no attempt to reproduce the rhyme-scheme.

—Brian Stableford

The Enchanted Ring
A Romance of Chivalry

I
The Two Talismans

IN the time of Charlemagne, long before he was Emperor of the Occident,[1] a beautiful and good princess, whose name was Libania, lived in the most marvelous and most isolated of the isles of the Orient. She was of the royal blood of Persia, but had exiled herself voluntarily from that land. We shall know the reason for that voluntary exile shortly.

A few years after her arrival on the island, one day when she was walking in its delightful promenades, she chanced to discover the entrance to a grotto previously unknown to her. Moderately curious, she crossed the threshold and ventured into a natural gallery decorated with little multicolored stones, petrifactions, corals and saxatiles. After walking for a few minutes she found a room of octagonal form, the walls of which were clad in

---

1 Charlemagne (742-814) became sole King of the Franks in 771 and Holy Roman Emperor in 800, so this implies that the tale is set in the 770s, although it owes its allegiance to Medieval Romance rather than to known history, which has many details in conflict with the story.

stalactites and crystallizations sculpted into facets, as if by the hand of a lapidary gnome. A soft and pure light, the source of which remained invisible, illuminated the beautiful room magically. A bronze statue occupied the central point: a calm and grave statue that represented a seated aged magus holding a golden box on his knees. That old man, bronze though he was, had the air of a rather benevolent individual. He smiled at Libania, who was increasingly astonished, and he said to her in a tone of paternal remonstration:

"You've been long awaited, my dear child."

Libania made a gesture that revealed the utmost degree of surprise.

When she had succeeded in recovering her composure, she replied in a tone that was simultaneously firm and respectful: "What do you mean, father?"

"I mean what I say. I'm complaining of having waited for you for a long time, and I'm not wrong. I've been waiting for you since the beginning of the world."

"And why have you been waiting for me?"

"To recompense you, on the part of God."

"Recompense me? Me! What have I done to merit that?"

"Think hard."

"I can't discover anything. The more I examine, the less I can comprehend that human equity, and divine equity above all, might owe me any recompense."

"O truly implausible modesty! You are named, and you are, Princess Libania?"

"Undoubtedly, that's who I am."

"It isn't knowing who you are to misunderstand your worth. However, I'm not sorry to find such a humble misunderstanding; in you, it's only one virtue more. Since you've forgotten your great actions, I'll take the trouble to recount them to you, and I beg you to listen without too much impatience to your historic eulogy. I'll be simple and accurate; I won't take too long, and I won't get carried away, as people will get carried away a thousand years from now in the Academy of Political and Moral Sciences . . . a scantly sublime thing that will, alas, be invented.

"I'll begin.

"You're twenty-five years old, and you lived until the age of twenty without knowing that you were born a princess of the royal blood of Persia. Brought up in Persepolis, in the house and under the guardianship of Aguilar, an opulent magus, you regarded yourself, and everyone else regarded you, as the daughter of his brother Setoc, the famous general who died young in a battle. On the evening of the twentieth anniversary of your birth, while you were daydreaming in your favorite garden, you saw four Nubian slaves advancing toward you, who were carrying a parchment on a cushion of silver cloth fringed with opals. When the cushion was deposited at your feet, you realized that the parchment was a missive from your guardian, who had been absent for several days. You shut yourself in the most discreet of your boudoirs, well-shielded from importunate eyes, in order to read and meditate upon the missive at your ease, the importance of which you sensed vaguely. And, in fact, nothing was more serious.

"The letter said:

"*Libania, you are not my niece; you are the daughter of the unfortunate Ammon, our legitimate sovereign, so wickedly dethroned and assassinated eighteen years ago by the usurper who governs Persia today. A few magi and I are the only ones who know the secret of your birth; the rest of the world believes that Princess Libania, the only child of the defunct monarch, perished in the conflagration of her father's palace, and that you have nothing in common with her but your name and age. Forgive me for having waited until now to make you this revelation. That is because, before telling you that you were born for the throne, I wanted to be sure of being able to conduct you to it. Now, I have the assurance of that; I have a party in the army; all the priests are with me; the people are discontented and I have a great deal of gold. Thus, your reign can begin whenever you wish. I will come back the day after tomorrow from a voyage undertaken in the interest of your accession. We will talk about the great objective. You will deign to explain your designs to the foremost of your servants and the one you have venerated for a long time as your father's brother. You are too generous and too honest ever to forget that, although God has put into you the seeds of all the qualities that make illustrious monarchs, it is to my cares as a sage guardian that you owe their entire development. It is me who has completed the work of God by giving you an education a thousand times higher and broader than that ordinarily given to the women of the Orient; so I hope that you will not hesitate to repose the conservation of your reign on the devoted arm that was able to found it for you. In that hope, I put myself at the feet of Your August Majesty.*

"Such adventures could not fail to disturb your mind. It is natural to have vertigo when, believing that one is marching in a plain, one suddenly perceives that one is treading on a summit. First, there was a chaos of confused impressions and formless ideas within you, a mixture of contrary designs and enemy desires. Soon, however, under the influence of reason, and the inspiration of justice, your soul calmed down, like the sea under the blue of the sky and the gold of the sun. Just and reasonable, you conceived a project that emanated exclusively from those two merits, and you spent half the night preparing its execution.

"The next day, at dawn, you abandoned your guardian's palace and Persepolis in the greatest mystery, only taking with you a dozen slaves and five dromedaries, serving for the transportation of a light baggage and a modest treasure. You left in your room a letter in response to Aguilar's. It said:

"*I do not want to reign, my dear Aguilar. I am leaving, and quitting the kingdom. I am hiding the place of my retreat from you, and I will take measures to prevent you from discovering it. If I am refusing the throne, do not think that it is for reasons of self-mistrust or modesty. Not at all; I confess to you ingenuously that I believe myself to be simultaneously strong and good, intelligent and simple: precious faculties whose assemblage, which is very rare, constitutes a truly royal character. I do not judge myself, therefore, to be unworthy. The motives for my refusal are otherwise. They are these. I do not want to reclaim my rank because I do not want to trouble the wellbeing of the people with a revolution—the wellbeing, you hear! When you say that the people are unhappy and discontented, you want to deceive me or to deceive yourself. Yes, the people are happy, very happy, and that is thanks to the sagacity and benevolence of the usurper. That tyrant, as you call him, is an excellent king. People admire him and love him. I know that with the aid of priests and the army you could easily achieve your violent aim, seduce the nation and restore the crown of my ancestors to me. But for that to be accomplished, how much blood and now many tears would have to be shed! Public felicity, you might reply to me, would only be interrupted; the excellence of my reign, which would equal the previous one, would soon return it. That is probable. But that interruption, however rapid you suppose it to be, would be an unpardonable crime, and would inflict an inexorable remorse upon me. Since I can only mount the throne by interrupting public felicity, I shall not mount it, even if I only had to interrupt it for a single day, or a single hour.*

"Oh, if the present king had personally dethroned and assassinated my father, then filial piety would order me to exercise a just vengeance and legitimate reprisals, but that is not the case; that is no more true than the discontent of the people. My father was not dethroned by an individual, by an isolated hostility; it is the nation as a whole that, in a fit of unanimous anger, rose up against his power and broke it. That anger, alas, was only too excusable: bad ministers, profiting from the sovereign's weakness, had governed oppressively in his name and rendered it odious to his best subjects. My father did not die under the thrust of an assassin; no one in isolation was the cause of his death; he fell gloriously, weapons in hand, in the struggles of the revolt, in the midst of a phalanx of faithful soldiers.

"After the victory of the insurrection, the great men of the realm, who had all participated in it—including you—assembled to draw lots to determine who would be king. The lot fell to the present king, and has not made a paltry present thereby to the human race. That good prince unites with the merit of governing well the even greater one, in my eyes, of not have robbed or murdered my father. You see, Aguilar, by the justice of my historical corrections, that I know fundamentally and in their true light the various events to which you refer. That perfect knowledge I owe to the education you have given me, to the 'education a thousand times higher and broader than that ordinarily given to the women of the Orient' I thank you, venerated magus, for having brought me up in a manner not to be the dupe of men or things.

"Joking apart, my dear guardian, I am grateful to you for your zeal and your cares, and I shall often have pleasure in thinking about you in my voluntary exile; for, in truth, you are amiable, generous and benevolent, although devoured by ambition. Adieu, then, my dear Aguilar. I release you forever from your oath of fidelity to my monarchical rights. Rally honestly, you and your followers, to the cause of the illegitimate king. I guarantee that he will appreciate you and will heap you with honors, as much as I could have done. Be for him what you would have been for me. Your legitimate queen commands it, and your affectionate ward implores it.

"That, word for word, is your letter, is it not? An ideally sage and noble letter, such as no child of a princely race has written before, or ever will write!"

"Is it for that, then," said the heroine, who was dying of impatience and had tried to interrupt the statue twenty times over, "for this exile and that letter, that you are charged by God with recompensing me?"

"Yes, my daughter, and I engage you to accept it with a good grace."

"Oh, don't worry. In spite of having all the trouble in the world persuading myself that I have merited this divine recompense, I am ready to receive it with delight. I love God with all my soul, and it is an unexpected joy for me to learn so positively that he is aware of it."

The statue opened the golden casket that it was holding on its knees, and, showing Libania two rings that it contained, it said: "Here are two inestimable talismans. One, which is made of solid mercury, renders invisible; the other, which is simply made of gold, inspires amour. Which will be fortunate enough to please you? You have the choice."

Blushing and slightly confused, but nevertheless without hesitation, Libania took the ring of amour.

"Aha, my beautiful solitary," said the old man, with a smile full of benevolent malice, "we foresee, it seems to me, that matters of the heart will be the great affairs of your life!"

"And we are very glad," said the princess, with a cheerful dignity, "to acquire in a manner so prompt and so sure the power to treat those great affairs greatly!"

The old man started to contemplate her with a strange expression of admiration; his gaze—a true gaze, although projected by eyes of bronze—venerated and deified her.

"Do you know, my daughter" he cried, in a passionate, enthusiastic voice, "that you are quite perfect and quite divine, for a human creature?"

That ecstasy and that madrigal appeared to be so exaggerated to Libania that she wondered for a moment whether the charm of the ring, which was already shining on her finger, was not operating on the metallic old man and rendering him amorous of her.

The statue responded to her thought.

"Be reassured," it said, "I have all my reason. If I redouble my eulogy in your regard and praise you with a new fervor, it is logically and justly, because a further meritorious trait has just escaped your person . . ."

"Oh, my good father," said Libania, with a gaiety mingled with impatience, "denounce that magnificent trait to me quickly, and after that, let us be silent once and for all, I implore you, on the subject of my glories."

"I have, therefore, to denounce to you," said the old man, "the elevation of sentiment that made you choose the ring of amour in preference to the ring of invisibility."

"But what is elevated about that? I obeyed the most ordinary instinct of my sex. Is not the sovereign good of women to love and to be loved? In my place, any other woman . . ."

"No, my daughter, no. In your place, the majority of women would have chosen the other talisman. It is true that to feel, and above all to inspire, amour is the principal ambition of female hearts; I grant you that. But there are extremely few women who, put in a position to decide for one of the two rings, would not have made the following reflections: 'I have beauty, grace and intelligence—charms, in sum—and hence the wherewithal to attract an honest number of suitors to my footsteps. What is important in the matter of amour is not to render myself lovable—I am that already—but to possess the means of domination, of knowing everything and being able to do anything. It appears to me that a part of that result ought to be obtained with the ring that renders invisible, and I shall take it!'

"Yes, all, I repeat, or almost all, would speculate thus. One can count those who, in your example, want to be loved for the sake of being loved, not for being obeyed, who do not wish to degrade amour to the point of making it the vizier of pride. Eternal praise to the grandeur of your soul, which has not permitted you the horrible paltry and vainglorious thought: 'One attraction more would be useless to me; I have enough of them; I shall be loved enough.' And yet, to what woman is it more appropriate than you to esteem herself sufficiently provided with charming qualities? You, who have the whiteness of doves, the eyes of a gazelle, the perfections of the goddaughters of fays, and on top of all that, the most grandiose air that ever a daughter of man obtained from God!"

"Of all the marvels that I have been able to see and hear since entering this grotto," said Libania, "none has surprised me more than the bizarre combination presented by the vivacity and warmth of those compliments with the immobile and cold nature of the bronze gallant who is pronouncing them."

"Immobile?" said the statue, and stood up, drawing itself up to its full height, not without a notable metallic resonance. It took a step forward. Libania took two backwards, stimulated by a slight and very understandable fear.

"Cold!" added that statue—and a flame sprang from its head. That flame, running all along its limbs and upper body, rendered the bronze malleable, agitated and stirred it like a floating robe of watered silk, and caused the sonorous envelope to fall away abruptly. A beautiful archangel, in all his superhuman splendor, was radiant before the amazed and delighted Libania.

"Well, my sister," he said, in the most celestial voice, approaching her and taking her hand, which he kissed, "do you still accuse my nature of coldness and immobility?"

"No; I accuse it much more of effervescence and indiscretion," said Libania, withdrawing her hand gently.

"How do you expect me to moderate the evidence of my gratitude, when your adorable advent has put an end to my captivity, broken my baleful enchantment and permitted me to ascend to the heavens again?"

"What had you done, then, beautiful archangel, that necessitated such an expiation?"

"I was steeped in the blackest of crimes; I had participated in the great revolt of the ingrate angels, the ideal catastrophe whose reality is recognized by all religions, even the least true. The inferiority of my temporal punishment, compared with the eternal torture of other genii, tells you that my participation in their crime was not absolute. In fact, during the last battle that we fought against the faithful angels, I felt troubled by vague remorse several times, and when, after our defeat, tumbling thunderstruck through space, we began to endure the gigantic fall that lasted nine days, I was horrified by the hardening of my vanquished brothers, whose pride was increased, instead of being humiliated, by our disaster.

"I was humiliated! I repented with all the force of my conscience, and I sent toward God one of the immeasurable sighs of distress that never strike his ears in vain. Then I stopped in the void, almost pardoned, and my unfortunate companions completed their descent into the infernal abyss without me. Then I wandered in desolate and tenebrous limbo until the day of the creation of worlds, a memorable day when the will of God put me on this earth, in this grotto, imprisoned in this bronze. He confided the two talismans to me and showed me on the distant horizon of the future the perfect woman whom I was charged with recompensing, and who, in return, was to operate my deliverance. Oh, that future! How long it has taken to become the present!"

"And confess, celestial genius, the haste you are in for it to become the past. How eager you are, are you not, to fly to the stars and to find yourself in your natal light again!"

"Yes, my sister, oh yes, although for that, it is necessary for me to quit you. But the least terrestrial of the daughters of earth would not be astonished that one should prefer Heaven to her, when one knows it. Oh, if I did not know it, could I imagine anything more desirable than the place where you are, than the sight of you?"

"Are the other archangels on high as gallant as you?"

"Oh, I cannot say anything about things up there!"

"Instruct me, at least, before departing, as to one things down here that is very important to me. Tell me how the virtue of my ring functions, and what are its particularities."

"Gladly. For as long as you do not love anyone amorously, for as long as you do not experience that exclusive sentiment under the empire of which one no longer sees any but one creature in creation—a state of the soul that, in a great future century, among a great people, a woman of genius will be born,[1] who will call it *egotism à deux*—for as long as you are animated by a calm and vast benevolence toward vast humankind, your ring will inspire, not only in humans but all animals, plants and the elements, the most miraculous benevolence in your regard. Thus, for you there will no longer be any malevolent people, ferocious animals or poisons; you will have nothing to fear from water, air, earth or fire. It will even enable you to realize the desire to travel that sometimes afflicts you, for you are terribly bored on this island."

"That's true," said Libania

"However," said the archangel, "as soon as your heart is absorbed in another, and the rest of the world no longer has the finest perfume of your sympathies, your relationship with creation will revert to the ordinary laws; animate beings and inanimate things will be liberated from the influence of your ring; it will only be exerted between you and your lover. It will be reciprocal; the talisman will assure you of him, and he will be assured of you. In his eyes, there will be no other woman but you, in your eyes, no other man but him. There will never be obstacles to your union, never a dolorous absence, never any suspicions, jealous apprehensions and never, never any satiation or cooling, but always, always happiness."

"What more can there be in Heaven, then?" cried the ecstatic princess.

---

1 Madame de Staël (but the attribution is a trifle uncertain).

"More? Perhaps nothing. But there is something less
. . . death!"

As he spoke, the archangel had opened his wings. He
rose a few inches above the ground, hovered momentarily
in mid-air, and then he leaned over toward the princess
with a chaste languor and kissed her on the forehead.

"Adieu, handsome archangel!" said Libania, still thinking about his last remark.

"Au revoir, my sister," said the handsome archangel.

The vault split apart, delivering passage to his flight,
which plunged into the ocean of the skies.

II
The Camp of the Avars

A S the genius had foreseen, the Princess of Persia traveled. First she visited the radiant, torrid Orient, sometimes, in its vital and fecund magnificence; sometimes in its sterile and mortal grandeurs; sometimes in its marble cities, its baths and palaces, its temples and its peoples, mantled in silk and crimson, the delights of its gardens, the cedars of its mountains, the nests of bulbuls, the fields of roses, the opulent limpidity of its rivers and the majestic voluptuousness of its woods; sometimes in the horror of its solitudes, in its deserts, its infinite expanses of sand, its taciturn necropolises, its volcanoes, its asphaltic lakes, the lairs of its alligators, the roars of its tigers, the hissing of its snakes, its tribes of marauding Arabs—and everywhere, the influence of the ring was notoriously manifest: much benevolence on the part of humans, no malevolence on the part of beasts, and no inclemency on the part of the elements.

Libania became the object of the most royal and chivalric attentions of Caliph Haroun-al-Raschid, and traversed without a shadow of danger the estates of the

Prince of the Assassins. She was able, in all security, to examine the pelts of lions and the eyes of reptiles at close range, and assailed with impunity on the terrible lake of Gomorrah. It was with an extreme delight that her affectionate soul traveled that immense spectrum of sympathies, and she scarcely had any desire to take a lover who would dispossess her of it.

Now she is in the Occident, in the heart of Germany, in the confines of the lands of the southern Slavs. In addition to the curious need to compare the solemn religiosity of the Germanic forests with the voluptuous majesty of Oriental forests and to search in the changing spectacle of a horizon blurred by cloud, vapor and mist, and some relaxation for a gaze fatigued by the monotonous aspect of a constantly blue and gold sky, a great thought, a noble desire, has attracted her to the regions of Europe; she wants to see and know the famous nation of France and its famous King Charlemagne. There is no corner of Asia in which she has not heard the king of that nation praised. A glory having such distant echoes has caused her to marvel profoundly.

Across an immense country, still half-savage, overflowing with potent vegetation, beneath a summer sun that puts everything in the lush landscape in relief. Libania, surrounded by her little caravan of servants, is riding rapidly northwards. The reason for that haste is that she wants to catch up with Charlemagne's army, occupied for a long time in this region making war on the Avars,[1] an

---

1 The Franks fought a series of campaigns against the Avar Khanate in the 790s. Historically, it was not Charlemagne but one of his sons who captured the fortified camp known as "the Ring" in which

adventurous and bold people whose fashions of making war are reminiscent of the ancient Parthians.

Until now, those indefatigable horsemen have thwarted the superiority of the strategic operations of the heroes. Skillfully alternating the impetuosity of attack and the rapidity of flight, they have worn down in their deserts strong legions of Franks, who have striven in vain to grasp and ungraspable enemy, and who encounter nothing anywhere but damp plains, marshes and overflowing rivers.

Today, Charlemagne has finally succeeded, not in vanquishing them, but in encountering them. He is holding them besieged in their camp, a retreat undiscoverable until now, so labyrinthine are the surrounding Hungarian forests. The camp is a prodigious wooden village that covers an entire province, enclosed by hedges of interlaced trees and flanked by marshes full of traps. It is between twelve and fifteen leagues around, like the vanished cities of the old Orient, such as Tyr, Nineveh, Babylon and Thebes of the Hundred Gates.

Certainly, the position is good, but no one would judge it impregnable and the camp of the besieged cannot without folly hope to dissolve, at length, the camp of the besiegers. However, the Avars would have had more chance of salvation if, persevering in their ordinary tactics, they had abandoned their wooden city, set fire to its huts and only confided themselves to the maneuvers

---

much of their booty was accumulated. According to the *Annales Regni Francorum*, attributed by legend to Bishop Tilpin (the Turpin of *The Song of Roland* and other romances), the Avars capitulated in 796, after which they were Christianized.

of their horses. That prudent course has been openly discussed among them, but it has not been adopted, for invisible attractions bind them to that soil and fix them in that place.

How could they resolve to quit, burn and lose that precious camp, the container of an accumulation of uncountable wealth? There are treasures several centuries old there, of several peoples; the spoils of the southern Slavs and Byzantines; a bizarre accumulation of the most sparkling and sumptuous objects, masterpieces of grandiose luxury, all things quite useless to those barbarians and harmful to the independent complexion of a nomadic tribe: the dream of a second-hand dealer realized, an incoherent museum of pillage.

That hoarding character, that mania of coveting gold, is doubtless what has earned those adventurers the name of Avars,[1] which surely cannot have been their original name, unless it was established by a rare mystery of predestination. On that point, as on many others, history remains silent, but the matter is serious. I propose to make it a subject for debate as soon as I am appointed a member of the Académie des inscriptions et belles-lettres.

Libania and her retinue are already among the tents of the besiegers. There, as elsewhere, the magic ring has had its effect. The princess has been welcomed at the entrance to the camp exactly as if her arrival had been foreseen. Her rank appeared no more dubious than her merit. A vague rumor had preceded her, announcing the appearance in the country of a process allied with the great

---

1 *Avares*, the French term for the tribe known in English as Avars, is coincidentally identical to the French word meaning "misers."

Haroun-al-Raschid, a rumor that spread all the more easily because its source was unknown and mysterious. She had been admitted and saluted as such; Charlemagne's peers, barons and seigneurs come to compete in offering her courtesy.

She strolls complaisantly in the midst of that swam of valiant and generous men, in the front line of which shine Duc Naimes de Bavière, the four sons of Aymon, their cousin Maugis, Roland, Olivier, Archbishop Turpin, Léon de Frise, Ogier the Dane, Richard of Normandy and many others no less celebrated.[1] She soon demands the honor of contemplating Charlemagne himself; after the satellites, she wants to see the star.

She is told that the meeting cannot take place before tomorrow, the king remaining enclosed in his tent in order to meditate plans of attack at leisure and having forbidden anyone to disturb his speculations for the whole day and night, on pain of exile. More than one knight hastens to offer to brave that royal prohibition on her behalf, and to assure her that, far from being annoyed by that importunate individual and punishing him severely, Charlemagne will thank him and even recompense him when he knows the reason for the importunity; naturally, however, she refuses, and we would expect no less of her noble politeness and her zeal in never allowing anyone else to take risks for her.

She continues to roam the camp, observing its physiognomy and character. The best order and discipline

---

1 The names not familiar in *The Song of Roland* are taken from the second most popular Medieval romance featuring Charlemagne's knights, *The Four Sons of Aymon.*

reside there: an order without stiffness and a discipline without rigor, because its principal motive is the enthusiasm of the army for its leader. How much intelligence and determination that leader has required to make the different races that compose the army adhere together solidly and to settle any disputes! It is not only the Franks and Gauls who have furnished the troops ranged under Charles's flag; Normans, Bretons, Belgians, Celtiberians, Lombards, Florentines, Saxons, Dalmatians and Danes have also requested and obtained the honor of serving as instruments for his bellicose projects. It would be appropriate to apply to him the two magnificent lines that Napoléon and his cosmopolitan bands inspired Victor Hugo to write: *One sees marching in his army / An entire people of nations.*[1]

That order, that harmony, the broad and picturesque symmetry of the tents that extend and interlace their alignments, the standards and banners that float superbly, the granular diversity of the costumes in which sumptuousness is only displayed on condition of being exclusively military, the iron and steel of the lances, the shields and the sabers that continually exchange flashes with the sun, all electrify, transport and excite Libania, inflaming the generosity of her blood and communicating to her nerves the sublime impatience of Arab chargers. She dreams of the intoxications of battle; she senses her soul being carried away by the turbulence of the melee. She hears in advance the clash of arms, and the din of fanfares. Her imagination displays for her the pomp of victory,

______

1 The lines are from "Les Deux Îles" in *Odes et ballades* (1826).

fascinates her with the pride of trophies and enables her to pass beneath triumphal arches.

Then, her saintly womanly pity and her elevated intellectual reason react, and those surges of heroism gradually calm down and die away. She begins to think dolorously about the horrors of carnage, to deplore the misfortune of mothers, wives and children. She sees the battlefield strewn with cadavers, still warm, wounded men moaning under the bellies of fallen horses. Arms, legs, torsos, hands and heads lie dispersed in the bloody grass. She hears the cries of despair and the maledictions of decimated families erupting from towns and the countryside. She is disgusted by the miserable fury of killing one another, which renders humans the image of beasts more than their faculties of loving and thinking render them the image of God.

Oh, that is because our Libania unites all the grandeurs of the human soul! How contradictory they are, how they tend to exclude one another mutually! The exaltation of courage, and its opposite, the detestation of murder, are both virtues! It is good to be brave, to be animated by warrior gusto, and it is also good to find war horrible, to desire peace! One is only complete if one possesses both sentiments at the same time! Humiliate yourselves, then, explicators!

However, Libania is distracted from these preoccupations by a man who emerges from the king's tent. He is a knight of tall stature, whose visor is mysteriously lowered, and whose proportions are absorbed by a long and ample blue velvet cloak. He walks with a grave and taciturn tread; he strides, traversing the streets of the camp. Everyone is astonished by his passage. "Who is he?" people say. "Where is he going?" But no one has the indiscreet temerity to interrogate Charles's messenger. Everyone knows, in any case, that there would be no profit in daring to do so, that no response would be accorded to the interrogator.

"Seigneur," says the princess to Archbishop Turpin, who is standing beside her, "can you divine who that man is, in spite of his lowered visor? Can you recognize him, or at least suspect who he is by his gait and his stride?"

"No, Madame. He affects the stiff and austere march of monks, and the amplitude of his cloak completes the concealment of his appearance."

"But see, he is passing the limits of the camp. He's in the grassland that separates us from the besieged city."

"Evidently, Madame, he is going to see the Avars. He is doubtless a secret ambassador of our august sovereign."

"I confess, Seigneur Prelate, that I have an extreme desire to visit the Avars. I have been told such original stories about their accumulation of riches."

"Well, Madame, seize the opportunity. With your palfrey, you will soon catch up with the blue knight, who is on foot. Inform him of your desire; without a doubt he will offer to share with you the safe conduct with which he must be provided."

Libania was about to reply that she had no need of a safe conduct, but she reflected that it was necessary not to say or do anything that might give the slightest indication of the existence of her talisman.

"You're right, Monseigneur," she said, "and I shall follow your advice."

"Right? I don't know. To venture among those barbarians on the simple faith of a safe conduct is quite hazardous. Would it not be wiser to wait until the city is in the power of the Franks?"

"What assures us that it will have kept its originality? How do you know that your Franks will not have disfigured it by putting it to sack, fire and blood?"

"That's true. Go, then, valiant heroine, and may God watch over you."

"Don't worry, Monseigneur. God will protect me."

The princess spurred her horse ardently and, accompanied by two slaves, headed toward the open ground that the blue knight was traversing.

Turpin watched her draw away with a melancholy gaze. "Of what God are you speaking, alas?" he said. "It isn't mine, who can do anything; yours is false and can do nothing. That poor princess, however, is not naturally impious; she even has religious instincts . . . either I'll lose my archiepiscopal science trying, or I'll convert her."

Meanwhile, the blue knight has turned round at the sound of the gallop of the mounted individuals running after him. At the sight of Libania he stops, surprised and charmed. He has not yet had the idea of such a great appearance, or a similar beauty. One of the slaves approaches and explains to him what the princess desires. Delighted by the opportunity thus presented to oblige the young marvel, the knight advances toward her with a gallant precipitation, and swears to her ardently that he is and will henceforth be as devoted to her as to Charlemagne.

The princess is not discontented by the effect she has produced, but as her modesty is unalterable she attributes all the glory of it to her ring.

"In truth, Madame," said the knight, "I feel sorry for the King of France. How did his gentlemen not divine that respecting his order to leave him alone, when it was a matter of introducing you to him, was to betray him while thinking to serve him? It was to deprive him of a contentment, to steal a joy from him."

"Permit me, Sire, to say that the gallant seigneurs did, indeed, believe that they divined that. It was me who did not consent . . ."

"Ah! It's you who have voluntarily adjourned Charlemagne's satisfaction," said the unknown man, with a singular tone of reproach and regret.

"Mine even more than his," said Libania, "for the sight of an illustrious monarch whose renown fills the world, is far more satisfying than that of a woman, even if that woman . . ."

"You're mistaken. A creature of God who has your perfections is even better to contemplate than the foremost hero on earth. That is the king's opinion."

"Oh, I know that your king is a passionate admirer and servant of the ladies. It's claimed that he merits being nicknamed the Solomon of the Occident."

"Please believe that there is a great deal of hyperbole in that nickname."

"I believe it willingly. I'm certain that, in his gallantry, Charlemagne has less universality and more elevation than the sage Solomon. In addition, I congratulate him in not having the latter's two great faults, slackness and indolence."

"Madame, do you know the features of the King of France? Have you ever seen an image representing him?"

"Yes. I possess a portrait of him that is the work of a painter of Byzantium. The painting is said to be very accurate."

"How do you find him, then?"

"As noble as his blood, as handsome as his genius."

An indefinable shudder agitated the blue knight beneath the amplitude of his cloak. He put his hand to his visor as if to raise it, but he seemed to reflect . . . and did not lift it.

The conversation resumed. It became serious and ingenious. It rose to touch great ideas and great sentiments. An equal exchange was made of well-thought and well-sensed ideas, which encountered one another with the name force. They were mutually convinced of one another's superiority.

The unknown man said to himself: *I don't know of any woman in Europe whose sagacity has half the perfume of this flower of Asia.*

Libania said to herself: *Such a man must Charlemagne's intimate friend and foremost adviser.*

While they were conversing, this is what has happened: the blue knight has shown his safe conduct to one of the guards stationed outside the city on the edge of the marshes that circle it. He has proved his quality as an envoy of the King of the Franks to the King of the Avars. As for the princess, needless to say, she would have been able to dispense with sharing the safe conduct; with regard to the besieged as well as the besiegers, the most favorable prejudices in her regard have been immediately produced.

Thus, she and the blue knight are now inside the barbarian city. Having paused momentarily at the summit of a high mount at its gates, which overlooks it, they scan it with their gazes, measure it, explore it and marvel at it.

Veritably, it is a strange and entirely novel spectacle that they have before their eyes.

Over the entire extent of the ground that the rampart of interwoven trees contains within its enclosure, long irregular lines of wooden huts, painted in many colors, extend and intersect, unfurl and curl, like the branches, knots and serpentine coils of a fabulous maze. An indescribable pell-mell of precious furniture, opulent fabrics and treasures, is thrown, strewn and spread over the earth; it is deployed and reigns over the entire length and breadth of the camp, through all the pathways, all the alleyways, all the streets and all the roads. The gaze grows weary and troubled in trying to enumerate and evaluate that gigantic accumulation of riches.

Scattered here and there are gold and silver vessels, bronze tripods, crimson veils, scarlet robes, fur coats, silk tunics, mosaic marble tables, pearly satin scarves, porphyry and jasper urns, crystal and alabaster amphorae, agate cups encrusted with gems, sculpted silver and bronze basins, solid gold beds, bouquets of diamonds, paintings by celebrated painters, sculptures by famous sculptors, and even books—yes, even books, scholarly and literary manuscripts copied by skillful calligraphers, bound by expert artisans and contained in cedar and sandalwood caskets . . .

And all that, we repeat, is mixed up, entangled, confused in the utmost disorder; clustered, compressed and compacted in such a manner as only to display very rare interstices over all its immense deployment. There scarcely remain, in the corners of the city, a few places to lodge the excellent horses that once enabled the success of the army, and which, alas, have become useless since it has been constrained to remain stationary.

The blue knight cannot help exclaiming: "With only a third of this prodigious booty, what great things, still in the state of speculation, Charles could effectuate for the wellbeing of his subjects and his personal glory!

"The race of men who live and move amid this clutter and animates its inert mass forms a contrast with him— or, to put it better, an absolute opposition. In fact, what is there in common between the luxury of an old civilization and these primitive, semi-savage natures, these tall and square statures, these abrupt heads whose chins nourish beards that rivals Gallic tresses in thickness and vigor, these broad and powerful breasts, these fleshy arms, these taut energetic legs that bring a sheaf of elastic and supple muscles into play at every step? Except for a few fabrics, a few jewels, a few utensils of feasting, men and women are unable to employ anything or assimilate anything of all this vast lumber-room in disarray. They tread upon it with brutal and ignorant feet. They are like deaf men in the midst of a collection of musical instruments. Their concern is not to use but to pile up, to sequester, to be able to say, proudly: 'This is ours!' They possess but they do not enjoy. Once again, whatever its origin might be, their name is well-acquired."

At the present moment, a notable agitation is circulating in the city. The moving disorder of minds is at least equal to the motionless disorder of material objects. The king of this people has just died suddenly, without any preliminary illness, as if struck by an invisible and mute thunderbolt. That unusual death is sowing superstitious dread far and wide with regard to the outcome of the war. Then too, it is necessary to elect a new king, and the great council of elders, which has assembled for that purpose, will encounter no small difficulty in the labor of that election. The defunct prince has left no direct heirs, no sons, brothers or nephews. There are only numerous and turbulent collaterals who are surrounding the royalty with the same covetousness, who all want to reign, and who are threatening rebellion against whichever of them is preferred to the others.

Naturally, the sage old men are trembling before that imminence of civil discord; they would be tempted not to name any of the competitors, and thus put them all in accord, but for that it would be necessary to have an elite individual to oppose to them who is far superior to them in birth and reputation and who could rally the unanimous suffrage of the multitude. Unfortunately, those competitors, without having any very profound merit, only count inferiors within the tribe.

The great council of elders sits patriarchally under the vault of the sky; it occupies a spacious circle that has been cleared in the midst of the heaped-up spoils. The Persian princess and Charlemagne's ambassador are introduced to it.

At first, the assembly's entire attention is exclusively devoted to Libania. When she appears, an admiring emotion is propagated like an electric current. There is not one of the old sages who cannot remember having been young and superb at twenty years of age. Her presence makes them feel what the presence of Helen made the elders of Troy feel in Homeric times. All of them have risen to their feet spontaneously, and the president, who is a centenarian, has indicated to her with a reverential gesture the place of honor—which is to say, a throne of sorts with an awning, normally employed by the sovereign, which is empty for the moment, since the dead king does not have a successor yet.

The French ambassador preoccupies the assembly in his turn. He has advanced into the middle of the circle with a dignity simultaneously free and urbane, still carefully masked by his visor and surrounded by the folds of his cloak. That mystery, that princely casualness, along with the idea of Charlemagne's grandeur floating in the air in the distance, earns the representative of that grandeur a certain tacit respect, and a silent approval.

He asks to speak. A sign is made that they are listening.

"Magnificent lords," he said, "I bring words of conciliation. My master, the king, desires peace, and I have come to propose to you on his behalf conditions that are not onerous. He will engage to cease all hostilities, to lift the siege of your city and to withdraw his armies from your territory promptly, provided that, for your part, you engage to make a pact of offensive and defensive alliance with him and to pay him an annual tribute of men and money . . ."

The word "tribute" was generally greeted with an arrogant frown and a bitter murmur.

The blue knight continued:

"Frankly, I scarcely understand your reluctance to shelter under Charlemagne's protectorate. Many nations have that honor, who do not cede anything to you in bravery or pride. Reflect, therefore. You are a valiant people, but you do not understand very much of the military art, the methodical defense of a fortress or the organization of a pitched battle. You only really shine in skirmishes, ambushes, fugitive and irregular struggles. Your former successes against us you have only been obtained in that fashion. What use is that kind of skill to you now? You can no longer practice it. This enclosure, which imprisons you, paralyzes your cavalry and constrains you to a mode of belligerence that is not yours. If you have the folly to persevere in your designs of resistance, you will soon succumb, in spite of the efforts of your admirable valor, for the besiegers possess in depth the part of the art that you lack; and furthermore, their number, already formidable, is growing from day to day and from hour to hour. It is, therefore, rather generous of the King of France to offer you peace and his amity on these facile conditions, and it can only be honorable for you to accept them."

The president replied: "Milord Envoy, the council of elders would surpass its powers if it made a decision, whether to refuse or to accept. According to our laws and customs, it is only the monarch who has the prerogative, among us, of concluding a treaty. When you arrived we were in deliberation regarding the choice of a new king. Would you please be kind enough to wait until it is terminated?"

"Very well!" said the blue knight. "But something causes me chagrin. The prince you are about to name ought to take his place on the throne immediately, and then he will be obliged to displace Madame"—he indicated Libania—"ungraciously and ask her to sit elsewhere. I suspect that, under that dais, the newly elected king, no matter how great he is, will not make a better figure than this charming princess. In my opinion, that unfortunate dispossession would constitute an event of very ill augury. It would, it seems to me, have something shady about it, which would have the odious appearance of a usurpation."

That singular speech—which made Libania laugh as if at a sally of humorous gallantry—appeared very serious to the assembly, and redoubled its gravity. The idea that it contained exercised upon them all the power of a sudden revelation. Each of them remained taciturn for a moment, motionless and absorbed, with a facial expression that seemed to say: "Yes . . . that's true . . . why not?" Then they all looked at one another, and smiled to see that everyone else had the same thought. A buzz of words spoken in low voices and whispers made a gradual tour of the circle of senators.

Libania, who felt that she was the focal point of all the words and gazes, was no longer laughing, because she understood.

Finally, after those mysterious negotiations, in which a half-compressed enthusiasm fermented, the president stood up with a solemn expression, quit his platform and, followed by the four principal members of the council, who were carrying the insignia of royalty, he marched straight to the royal dais where Libania was still enthroned. Emotion rendered her very pale when the scepter, the crown, the balance and the sword were deposited at her feet . . .

The five old men had bent their knees, and interminable acclamations burst forth, not only from the deliberating assembly but from all the people whom an anxious expectation had gathered around the perimeter.

Even the contenders played their part in that vast chorus of public adhesion. And it was genuinely with good faith and frankness that they applauded and acclaimed. Apart from the fact that the ring did not exempt them from its fantastic influence, the choice of the elders satisfied them for two positively excellent reasons: firstly because, none of them having supplanted his competitors, their respective jealousy did not have to bleed; and secondly because each of the ambitious men was fomenting and caressing in his soul the consoling hope of seducing and marrying the queen.

With a proud and mild gesture, the new queen announced that she wanted to speak. The multitude fell silent as one man, breathlessly, their silence as passionate as their cries.

"You want my reign . . . you shall have it. It will be difficult not to recognize the voice of God in your voice. My election has all the symptoms of a miracle. But think hard about this: I am from an Oriental land, the native soil of absolute power. I intend to govern you without division and without control. It will be necessary to obey me!"

A thousand acquiescent clamors responded. All mouths and hands made the oath.

46

"The first action of my sovereignty," Libania continued, "Will be to sign the treaty of alliance with Charlemagne. Nevertheless, Sir Ambasador," she added, addressing the blue knight, who bowed, "I will only consent to sign it if your master modifies it relative to the annual tribute. I judge the obligation of paying an annual debt to another people incompatible with the dignity of a valiant people. I will only admit a contribution made once and for all. Let the King of France renounce that clause and, in return, we will decide to abandon to him a third of the incalculable riches that are heaped up, dormant, in this city."

There was a faint whisper in the crowd. A haughty displeasure creased the queen's forehead.

"No murmuring! No criticism!" she cried. "Otherwise, I abdicate!"

A universal clamor of protestations of obedience returned serenity to her features.

Then the blue knight, who has maintained an impassive and neutral attitude thus far, advances toward the throne, and in a voice that resounds in such a manner that everyone can hear it, he says: "Great queen, honor and wellbeing to you! Charlemagne accepts the proposed modification, and it is him, in person, who declares it to you!"

While proffering those words, the pretended ambassador—who is in fact, none other than the magnanimous Charles—has lifted his visor and stripped off his cloak . . .

General amazement! The small number of those who know the hero repeat ecstatically: "Yes . . . yes . . . it's him!"

No less impressed than the crowd, Libania descends respectfully from her throne, compares from memory the original with the portrait, and silently renders homage to the fidelity of the latter.

Gazes do not weary of contemplating Charles's noble visage, and that is right, for his physical advantages are the perfect corollaries of his moral advantages. When one has genius, it does not spoil anything also to be handsome, tall and strong. Calm and activity are simultaneously legible on his noble face. In his nature, broad and fine, robust and ideal, there is a kind of combination of the pagan Jupiter and a Christian archangel; there is also the omnipotent rectitude of a plane tree combined with the svelte elegance of a palm tree.

Thus, the fortunate spectators have before them the most handsome of the men of the Occident and the most beautiful of the women of the Orient.

Noisy admiration soon replaces mute admiration, and that entire mass of people dissolves in explosions of cheers.

Charlemagne is escorted triumphantly back to his tents. Exorbitant virtue of the ring!—the news of the peace does not excite the shadow of a discontentment among the Franks, who were so exasperated against the Avars, so jealous to avenge on them the reiterated defeats of previous armies.

The following day, the king of the besiegers and the queen of the besieged conferred together and made their adieux.

Charlemagne obtained from Libania the promise that she would visit France as soon as she had extracted her realm from disorder and barbarity by means of her policed administration.

The Franks required fifteen hundred carts to carry away the share of the booty that the treaty conceded to them.

Libania, who had too much good taste to want to call herself Queen of the Avars, took the name of Queen of Transylvania, a land that formed a province of her Estates.

III
The Serpents' Egg

WE have crossed an interval of at least sixteen months. We find Charlemagne again in the south of his beautiful realm, retired to a palace neighboring the white Pyrenees, where he is employing the precious leisure granted to him by a momentary peace to stimulate the progress of the arts, organize civil order and redirect some of his capitularies.

Among the number of persons elevated in dignity who are sharing his residence, there are two who are giving him an assistance that is not mediocre in his legislatory task, so much do they know about the matter and so universal is their good advice. One of those two persons is Archbishop Turpin, the other Libania. The Queen of Transylvania has fulfilled her promise to visit the king and his realm at the end of a year. Her aptitude in reasoning affairs of State should not surprise the reader; a year of reigning has sufficed for her to understand the theory and practice fundamentally. In a year, she has regenerated her people and her territory; from barbarity she has engendered civilization; she has improved cities, mores and laws.

50

One of the skills that she has deployed with the most success is that of knowing how to divine elite men, attracting them to her and utilizing them. Now, that useful sagacity, after having been exercised fruitfully to her own profit, is being exercised with no less success to that of Charlemagne. At her instigation, the King of the Franks has just enriched his court with Clement of Ireland, the Anglo-Saxon Alcuin, Saint Benedict of Aniane, the Lombard Paul Warnefrid, the Visigoth Theodulf and the Spaniard Agobard, all men of high character and sublime understanding, who are working, under the eye of the master, to endow his subjects with flourishing intellectual and moral reforms

It goes without saying, given what we know of Libania's soul, that in the acts of her government she has always striven, before anything else, to be just and clement, and that, in her discussions with Charles she always preaches, as the two best secrets of the art of government, justice and clemency. Let us observe that all the true geniuses of politics and the science of the human heart have proclaimed the principle with one voice that an irreproachable rectitude is the most infallible of skills.

Archbishop Turpin, whom the eminent virtue of the Queen of Transylvania throws into a perpetual delight, applies himself assiduously to his ancient project of converting her. Every day, he talks to her about religious questions. He attacks her, he lays siege to her, he presses her with all his arguments of theosophy and philosophy; but he scarcely succeeds. He is dealing with a strong party. The pagan—or, rather, the unbeliever—is a consummate thinker. She is possessed of the most obstinate of evil spirits, the spirit of examination, which defends its possessions vigorously.

And yet, the good archbishop does not lose courage. He sometimes says to himself, in order to animate himself, what the great Corneille was to say eight centuries later in the beautiful line: "She has too much virtue not to be a Christian!"[1] In any case, he is sustained by a powerful auxiliary, a proven doctor, the foremost theologian of the epoch. That theologian is none other than Charles himself, who might have been as great a pope as he is a king.

As you can imagine, it is not uniquely the interest and glory of God that makes him share Turpin's apostolic zeal. You cannot doubt that our hero has fallen madly in love with our heroine, with a noble and pure amour, and that, if he wants her to be a Christian, it is very much in the interest of his happiness as a lover, being unable, without alienating his people, to take for a wife and place on the throne of France an enemy of God and the Church.[2]

The intrepid conqueror, the tamer of the Saxons, the vanquisher of the Germans, the Spaniards and the Lombards, has been vanquished, tamed and conquered in his turn. There is no Hercules who does not find his Omphale. The man intrepid in war is at present timid in amour, to the point of loving very quietly, desiring silently . . .

------

1 The quotation is from Corneille's drama *Polyeucte martyr* (1642). The eponymous character converts to Christianity, causing great anxiety to his wife Pauline, to whom the comment refers. A related quotation from the play is expanded later in the story.
2 The historical Charlemagne was already on to the second of his four wives before becoming king, and had several children.

Yes, the powerful Charlemagne is afraid. He has not yet dared to risk a word of confession.

And Libania? Is she in love? Does she perceive that she is loved? Neither one nor the other. Or, if she is in love, she is completely unaware of it. Her great purity of soul and the candid simplicity of her heart prevent her from having the idea of interrogating herself and examining herself on that subject. Her indifference is dubious, but her ignorance is certain.

Let us begin the recitation of an adventure that will soon awaken her and enlighten her entirely as to her veritable sentiments, and which will also furnish Charles's sentiment with the opportunity to manifest themselves and explain themselves.

One morning in July, which has begun full of radiance and smiles, Libania is walking alone in the gardens of the palace. She has no other objective than to allow her calm reveries to expand. At the corner of a bushy hornbeam hedge, she suddenly finds herself face to face with Charlemagne.

The latter, unusually, is in the costume of a simple archer: clothing that is singularly facile and convenient for the fatigues of marching and running, and for getting oneself out of a dangerous spot briskly. A page is holding a beautiful horse by the bridle, which he seems to be ready to mount. At the appearance of the Queen of Transylvania he shudders. He is disconcerted; he lowers his eyes and blushes.

Libania is astonished. She is embarrassed by her reaction to the embarrassment that she sees in him.

Finally, the king pulls himself together, looks at her, and says, cheerfully: "I look guilty, do I not. And, in fact,

I am disposed to be. You've surprised me at the moment of going to commit a great folly."

"Seigneur," she says, "it's so much the better that you have some shame. The prudence of your friends ought at least to dissuade you from this foolish enterprise."

"Well, yes, Madame, I do have some shame. But I have even more chagrin at not having been able to effect my departure without being seen by one of those friends of whom you speak. It only lacks my friend the archbishop to appear now. As you might imagine, it was you and him, above all, whom I trembled to encounter."

"That signifies, does it not, that you support impatiently the best criticism in the world touching your design, resolute as you are not to submit to it?"

"Frankly, I will hold to my project, heart and head. It is something I desire, as I am able to desire. Nothing can make me renounce it: nothing! Not even—dare I say it?—an insistent plea from your mouth . . . and yet . . . you will be generous. You will refrain from using your power. You will not try to put a yoke on my ardent whim."

"Perhaps. First of all, have the complaisance to name and identify for me the object in question."

The king takes from his pocket a book, small in form, bound in violet velvet, ornamented on the spine and boards with triangles of fine pearls. It is a book of sorcery.

"Here, Madame, read this," he says, presenting it to Libania, open, and designating a paragraph to her.

The queen reads aloud: "No talisman equals the one known as the serpents' egg. It has the virtue of rendering one invisible, aiding one to know the future, unveiling the thought of one's neighbor, and protecting well beyond the ordinary term youth and health. It only operates all that in the hands and in favor of the man who acquires it at risks and perils.

"This is the place where it is found, how it is formed what it is necessary to brave in order to render oneself master of it:

"During the summer, in the moon of July, in a cavern of Gaul situated at the foot of the Pyrenees and on the shore of the Ocean, countless serpents assemble which, all day long, as a manner of pastime, mingle, intermingle, enlace one another, knotting and braiding, and with their saliva combined with the foam that emerges from their rutilant skin, compose that species of egg. When it is finished, perfect, complete and polished, they raise it up and sustain it in mid-air by means of their breath and their hissing.

"It is then that it is necessary to take possession of it before it has touched the earth. Then, the adventurous mortal who has had the temerity to station himself to that effect, must launch himself forward, receive the egg dexterously in a cloth embroidered with the arms of Phoebe, leap on to a waiting horse and draw away at top speed, flat out, for the serpents, foaming with rage will pursue him until he is able to put a river between himself and them, none of them being of a species or nature to live and move in the water."

Libania closes the volume and hands it back, calmly and pensively, to Charlemagne. "And you're going there?" she says, rather severely.

"I was about to . . ." he says, slightly confused. "And I'm going," he adds, quietly, but with a very determined air.

"You're right to call that a great folly. Has God given you the gift of courage in order to squander it in that fashion? Would dying in that escapade be dying nobly? Do you have the right to seek a danger of death, the objective of which is neither the glory of your reign nor the salvation of your people? Is it noble to gamble your life in order to gain a possession that will only profit you?"

"Oh, Madame, please, spare me! Do you think that I have yet to address those reproaches to myself? Nevertheless, I do not veritably merit the last of them. It seems to me that one of the advantages of the talisman would be reflected upon my people."

"Which one?"

"Have you not repeated to me often enough that I have the key to the vault of my subjects' happiness, and that my successors might succeed me, but cannot replace me?"

"Yes, of course. Well?"

"Well, since one of the properties of the magical egg is to prolong existence, always to maintain it young and strong, I would assure the wellbeing of my subjects by conquering a remarkable duration."

"Oh, you're having recourse to sophistry, you who once detested it and despised it so much."

"It's in order to prove to you that nothing will turn me away from my resolution."

"I can see that all too clearly, and I no longer want to reason against it. I shall shut up."

"Charming Queen, accord me more than your indulgent silence. Say prayers for me. Wish me success."

"With all my heart, Seigneur . . . and if I listened to it I would do even more; I might . . . yes, I would perhaps end up encouraging you, approving of you, for the spirit of adventure is contagious. And then, in truth, this enterprise has something original and ardent about it, which is seductive."

"Yes, Madame, something impassioning, bewitching! I'm excusable, am I not?"

"Oh, very excusable."

"Adieu, then, beautiful Queen. From now until sunset there are about ten hours. That is almost the sum of the time that the expedition requires."

"Seigneur, I do not accept your adieu."

"What?"

"Tell me, have you in the palace stables a mount worth as much as the one your page is holding?"

"Of course. Why?"

"Deign to order that it be saddled, bridled and brought to me."

"You're . . . going out? Alone?"

"Alone? No. I'm accompanying you, I'm in the expedition."

"Heaven! What are you saying?" Charles cries, impetuously, frightened and charmed at the same time: charmed by the idea that if Libania is demanding to accompany him, to share his perilous temerity, it is doubtless because she loves him; frightened by the idea that the serpents will pursue them, that they might seize her, that they might stifle her and perhaps tear her apart.

Libania only perceives his fear.

"Don't worry," she says. "I'm endowed with a talisman that neutralizes in my regard the malevolence of the most pernicious animals. Its privilege even extends to the persons with whom I am keeping company."

"And you're very sure of his talisman?"

"Very sure. Many a time, in my numerous voyages, I've had occasion to experience its efficacy."

Charles breathes. His fear is dissipated; his joy is doubled proportionately, for it is reasonably demonstrated to him that a sympathy more or less sister to his own exists in Libania. She has only abandoned her resistance to the project that is attracting him because she is conscious of being able to master the evil. She is not going with him in order to share his dangers but to nullify them. She no longer fears what he is asking of himself because she is certain of saving him. Oh, our lover can expand in hope without unreason. Thus, he does so in the depths of his soul, very quietly—for he is too noble and too worthy to do so overtly; and I swear to you that his discretion and his reverence have great difficulty in preventing his contentment from permitting itself some sudden external expression.

The king has summoned his page and has commanded him to go in quest of another horse as good as the one that is present.

The page returns with a charger that does not appear to be inferior to its colleague.

Already the King of France and the Queen of Transylvania are in the saddle. They escape quietly via the most covert and least frequented part of the garden and reach one of the secret exits.

All hail to the earth and the sun! Here they are, galloping over the fields.

Their first impressions are neither sentiments nor ideas, but good and broad sensations. Each of their organs is striving to perceive all the power of the great objects of nature, those of a blond light that vivifies and inflames, those of a smiling blue firmament that exalts and enchants, those of an abundant series of efflorescences and foliages that embalm and refresh. The vivid and harmonious movement of their course is like a circle of central attraction that brings those vivid harmonies toward them, invests them and incorporates them. They enjoy all that instinctively, like two children, with an impetuosity full of candor, without the intervention of examination or analysis.

They are feeling, and they are not observing their feelings; their minds are floating completely free from political and social matters, the artificial and conventional glories of the world; they no longer discern anything but the natural and real glories of creation. They no longer know that they were a king and a queen; they no longer know that there are such things as kings and queens. They no longer know anything, except that they have life and daylight, air and space, verdure and sap.

Gradually, however, their souls, which were glad to sleep in the rocking of that excitement like a fisherman in the bottom of his rapid boat, wake up, recognize themselves and collect themselves, and that gradual internal change has an external reaction. A little while ago, without having a coherent conversation, they were chatting frequently, they were sending and returning to one another animated and joyful words, frank and cheerful gazes, candid and affectionate laughter . . . they were neither reflecting nor thinking . . . an enviable condition! Now they are thinking and reflecting; reserve, if not embarrassment, rides between them. They no longer exchange any but briefly discreet words, interrupted by long silences, moderate and serious gazes, contained, almost grave smiles . . .

That is because each of them is specially and separately occupied with a distinct interest. Charles, in his ideal being, is solicited energetically by his amour, which has a great desire finally to declare itself, and will not consent to let such a fine opportunity to do so be lost. As for Libania, she is gripped by a strange perplexity; a troubling thought has just traversed her brain, in these terms:

Yes, yes, I'm very sure of my ring; it will subjugate and tame the serpents . . . I don't love anyone amorously . . .

You might wonder why we qualify that thought as troubling. It is because, beneath her apparent character of firmness and certainty, a vague and mutedly dubious emotion has slid. Libania would not be thinking of encouraging herself if there were no need. That need for encouragement, minimal as it is assumed to be, must originate from a sketched doubt. Now what can have inspired that commencement of doubt within her? What: the mysterious language of the elements in festival dress, to which she has lent a more attentive and more impressionable ear than usual. The mysterious language that has only one word and the superhuman music that has only one note—amour—have proffered their word

60

so eloquently and sung their note so melodiously that she has been stirred involuntarily . . . hence, the sudden impulse of assurance that thought it ought to respond to her emotion and which, far from belying it, has only observed and demonstrated it further.

She darts a covert anxious glance at Charlemagne, and she repeats to herself: *No, I don't love anyone amorously . . . not even him . . . What I feel for him is doubtless something profound and animated, but it's not that . . . My God, what if it were amour? Come on, let's see, let's have the courage to examine ourselves. What do I feel for him? An immense but not blind admiration; the immensity of his glory justifies it . . . an immense esteem that has nothing exaggerated; his daily acts of equity and wisdom motivate it highly . . . a strong and durable affection that is founded on everything that resides in him of the good, the humane, the generous, the faithful, the loyal . . .*

Is that amour? Are not almost all philosophers who have treated that passion in accord in saying that, among people of a firm and chaste nature, its advent is recognizable principally by an access of weakness that tends to replace their firmness, and intermittences of a shame that chagrins and frightens their chastity? Now, personally, I don't discover anything similar in myself. I have no shame or weakness. I see and I hear the king without disturbance and without blushing. No slavish sentiment is imposed on me by him. Thus, it isn't amorously that I love him . . . at the very most, it's an enthusiastic amity.

Thus she reasons, and she thinks that she is reasoning very logically, when Charlemagne, indicating a colossal clump of oaks and beech trees to her in the middle of the plain, proposes that they make a halt there.

"We're only a short distance from our destination now," he says. "It would be good for our mounts to rest for a little while. The extreme speed that we're going to require of them for our flight demands that they're entirely robust and fresh. Then again, I need to reread in the grimoire you saw the description of the vicinity of the cavern."

Libania gives her assent. Our pilgrims go to sit down in the broad shadows of the oasis.

The place is invested with a singular grandeur and majesty. The natural disposition of the trees, the order of their trunks, their branches and their foliage, forms a kind of colonnade alternated by arches and porticoes sustaining a cupola rich in amplitude and depth. In that monumental essence there is a false air of a temple, which edifices the heart and magnifies the imagination.

O puritans, preachers, casuists, rigorists and doctors of morality, all of you who anathematize poetry and poets, music and musicians, painting and painters, all arts and all artists, under the pretext that they are better distillers of the poison of amour, that they are the ultimate industry to cause the most superb hero and the least sensible heroine to fall into one another's arms, of what are you thinking, my masters, in not proclaiming a similar anathema against nature, against the spectacle of her beauties and her pomp, against the influence of her ardors, her perfumes and her attractions?

It is not enough, it is nothing, to forbid your flock novels, romances, verses, opera, ancient drama, modern drama, paintings and sculptures, if you do not also forbid them golden suns, azure skies, warm summers, lush forests and the effervescent aromas of the fields! In the role of counselors of tenderness, dragomans of amour, what are the former compared with the latter? Oh, doctors, I denounce nature to you as the procuress *par excellence*. The word is vivid, but, trust me, it is merited. Yes, the sun is immoral!

Nothing is more dangerous for two people worthy of one another and generously organized than to find themselves together, in a beautiful season, on a lovely day, in the bosom of a beautiful location, than to contemplate it together, than to be subject together to its mystery and its sovereignty, even if they are not alone, even if a third party, more or less imposing, more or less importunate, is walking or stationed with them. If there is already a hint of sympathy between them, the magnetism of nature will magnify it and will be able to complete it. If nothing of that yet exists, a seed of devouring passion will be sown that will not be aborted, which will ferment and develop inevitably.

Conclusion: If you want to extinguish amour, first extinguish the sun.

Soon, Charles and Libania are able to observe that the repose they have entered is more agitated than the movement that they have left behind. The elementary fluids, the quadruple fascination of sylphs, undines, salamanders and gnomes, reach them more immediately, envelop them and penetrate them more intimately. All of that rises toward them, descends over them, and gravitates around them, some from the long grass, tufted moss and limpid springs, some from the great sky and the great trees, and some from the sparkling circle of the distant horizons.

By that redoubling of animation in their minds Libania is alarmed—and Charles congratulates himself . . . he refrains from neglecting the advantage. He draws assurance and eloquence from it. This time, he speaks; he reveals himself; he confesses . . . not in a direct, positive and banal fashion—that poor taste is alien to him—but in an elegantly and ardently mysterious fashion, with a thousand blazing allusions tempered by respect and veneration. He is careful to evoke the memory of celebrated attachments, the images of poetic and historic lovers; he shows them religiously, he names and enumerates them piously, and behind the radiation of their apotheosis, he makes the apparition of his personal amour float distinctly.

Libania is very disconcerted. Involuntarily, her heart palpitates. She makes laudable efforts, it is true, to hide that emotion; she affects an inattentive silence, and errant, distracted gazes. She does better than that; to the appearance of intention and distraction she attempts to join the reality; she tries not to listen, to preoccupy herself with something else . . .

Fruitless attempts! She hears only too clearly, and is only too absorbed by what she hears. It is easy to detect there a symptom of significant weakness. In addition, blushes and modesties run from her head to her feet, the significance of which is no less. Then she disentangles from the confusion of her fantasy, and surprises in one of the corners of her soul I know not what muted and vague joy in being adored, which flutters like a sly sprite.

Those discoveries importune and exasperate her. She sees the reef; she understands quickly the urgent need to escape the wind that is impelling her—which is to say, the traction of Charles's speech. She stands up abruptly, whips the air with her switch and returns to her horse.

"Let's go, Seigneur, come on!" she says. "It's getting late and the horses have recovered. Let's go."

Charles obeys, not without having to dissimulate a deep sigh.

Instead of setting forth like that in order to fly more rapidly to the magical lair, another woman would stop and say to herself, fearfully: *My God, where am I going What delirium is mine? If I love amorously—which isn't possible—my ring will withdraw its safeguard! Frightful dangers await us, him and me! Him above all, the man whom, perhaps, I love! Oh, let's beg him to desist; let's intimate to him that it's necessary to turn back. Since he loves me so much, he'll grant my wish, he'll obey me. It's true that that would take away a sure and infallible means of delivering me rapidly from the doubt I have regarding the state of my heart, an uncomfortable and onerous doubt that hinders and wearies me. No matter: the annoyance of taking a long time to dissipate it, with security, is better than the satisfaction of clarifying it at a stroke by playing such a game.*

But the Queen of Transylvania is one of those prompt and willful souls of which patience is neither the virtue nor the fault, and who disdains constraining herself to untying, at length and methodically, a more-or-less Gordian knot, especially when they have in hand the wherewithal to cut through it neatly and curtly. The demon of her heart is unable to adapt to the fogs and undergrowths of uncertainty.

Thus, it is with a bold transport that she resumes riding toward the perilous cavern where her stormy doubt will infallibly receive a full and entire solution.

Assuredly, the interior voice of prudence does not fail to argue against the terrible hazards of the adventure; but to that she responds that she and Charles are equipped with all the necessary courage and composure; that fortune is their subject, that the horses are possessed of an Arabian celerity and intelligence; and that, in any case, the king, knowing the country perfectly, will not take long to interpose the savior rampart of a river between them and the serpents.

"We're close, are we not, Seigneur?" she says, with a sort of feverish urgency.

"Yes, Madame, we're almost there. Do you see, two hundred paces ahead of us, in that vague terrain studded with mounds, that legion of cacti in regular rows, displaying their beautiful red flowers so proudly? According to the itinerary, the cavern is in the center of that thicket."

"Those bright red flowers," says Libania, "precede in a curiously symbolic manner the bloody eyes of the dragons."

"Look, this is what announces more completely the lords of this place," said the king, showing her fragments of skeletons on the edge of the path, in a ditch, and, further away, a recent cadaver, utterly disfigured, soiled, excavated, torn apart and twisted . . .

The great queen turns her eyes away with an insurmountable horror. She shivers and goes pale. The great king, who had initially wanted not to cease being impassive, does the same. Well, what human flesh would not lose its impassivity in confrontation with that corpse, the ugliness of which is as infernal as Hell; that death compared with which the most mutilated and most frightful corpses on a battlefield after the action would see almost amiable and cheerful objects?

Charlemagne is on the point of asking Libania for a second time whether she is quite sure of her talisman . . . but he abstains, reflecting that she might misinterpret the true motive for the renewal of that question and suspect a moderation of courage where there is absolutely nothing but a tender solicitude for her.

On the other hand, it is as well that he abstains from his interrogation, for the necessity of replying to it would be very embarrassing.

Nevertheless, he plans to conduct himself as if the talisman merited some suspicion. He promises himself to be on his guard, to employ, above all, vigilance and circumspection.

While our adventurers pass into the midst of the bands of cactus, a good number of the flowers of those plants begin to open. Everyone knows, undoubtedly, that when those flowers open, they produce a veritable explosion. Those thunderous sounds burst forth as the temeritous couple pass by, and go toward the monsters, as if to honor them. Do they not compose an anticipatory parody of the artillery discharges that will, many centuries later, salute from the harbor walls of ports vessels departing for the hazards of the high seas?

Already, the rumor of the serpents, the murmur of their capers, can be distinguished: an extra-human, extraordinary, terrifying, indescribable rumor of which Sabbat banquets would be jealous.

The orifice of the cavern appears; it is spacious. It is a kind of formless arch constituted abruptly by superimpositions of rocks. It is easy for two persons on horseback to enter it riding abreast, all the more so as a broad path is frayed through the luxuriant vegetation that encumbers the soil. That clearing, which appears to be recently made, is immediately reminiscent of the unfortunate dead man, whose work it probably is.

Charlemagne dismounts under the vestibule of the cavern. He begs Libania not to imitate him, not to follow him, to wait there with the horses; but Libania refuses. Like him, she wants to see. She wants, above all, to take the same risks as him—and that she can doubt that she loves him amorously.

The sound of the serpents, which can now be heard in all of its sonority, announces that the theater of their games is the adjacent chamber.

Our heroes pass between the intermediary pillars.

Let us describe what they see.

An immense rotunda: an immense round basin hollowed out in the soil and bordered by a narrow and rugged margin; and in that basin, a thousand serpents of every species, every form, every dimension and every color, which are moving, undulating, floating, rolling and swelling, so tightly-packed, so heaped up and so entangled that one might think it a single monstrous network.

The scene is only illuminated by a faint and vague twilight emanating from a slight fissure in the vault.

That moving, foamy, undulating and noisy mass with a thousand black, gray, brown, green, bistre, yellow and violet heads flamboyant with the mobile streaks of blazing scarlet eyes, offers some resemblance to the nocturnal aspect of a turbulent gulf whose waters are reflecting, and disfiguring as they reflect them, the constellations of the night.

Meanwhile, the magic egg so dearly coveted is gradually appearing in the seething foamy conflict of the reptiles. It is rising up, as pure and as white as a vapor of the dawn. Triangular threads of gold interrupt the purity of its whiteness. It floats and oscillates in the atmosphere of the basin, borne on the breath of its authors, the serpents, which are swooning in delight and swelling up with pride at the sight of such a pure creation engendered by their filthy host.

Libania and Charles have the privilege of witnessing that spectacle with an extraordinary presence of mind and a marvelous calmness of flesh. Their gaze has all the lucidity indispensable to flee rapidly, if there is reason to do so. Facing mortal danger, elite souls always have nerves of steel.

The serpents do not perceive their presence, or, at least, are unworried by it.

Charlemagne holds himself ready on the extreme edge of the basin. He is watching for the moment when the egg, gently swaying in mid-air, moving back and forth, here and there, in all directions, will finally be pushed toward him. The cabalistic cloth is deployed in his hands, ready to receive the talisman.

His desires do not take long to prosper. The egg approaches, advances, and arrives . . .

At the risk of falling into the gulf, the king leans forward avidly, extends the cloth and receives it therein. He smiles and quivers in triumph, and precipitately seals his conquest in a little silver urn suspended from his belt.

The tumult of the serpents has suddenly ceased . . . but after a moment of profound silence and absolute immobility, the movement and the noise are reborn and resume, a thousand times more formidable. The two profaners—whose sentence is notified to them by the scarlet eyes and the venomous tongues—seizing one another by the hand, depart at the pace of Meleager and Atalanta, and in three bounds are on their horses.

Then the flight and the pursuit commence . . .

Horses and riders go, run, gallop, fleeing with all their will and all their might. They have only one idea, only one instinct: their salvation, their conservation. In each of them the will that reigns and the energy that acts are in accord, harmonizing marvelously, fusing with one another. Each horse is no longer anything but one with its rider; their duality is resolved into unity. The centaurs have returned.

A swarm of reptiles has hurtled out of the cavern. They are sliding, they are crawling, rearing up and ducking down, hastening, crests ardent, eyes agape, tongues darting, their skin scaly and vibrant. Nevertheless, even though they are employing full diligence, even though they are forcing their effort to the maximum, it is easy to see, from the firm liberty of their casual manner, the disdainful grace of their elegance, that they have the most excellent opinion in the world of their success, that they are certain of their prey.

And the two riders? Are they equally certain of their salvation? No . . . at least, not with the same degree of certainty. But that moderation of hope does not detract at all from the perfection of their flight. They expend therein all that they have of vigor, tenacity, skill and composure. They give proof of the most admirable courage. And do not allow that affinity of the words *flight* and *courage* to be judged extravagant here. There are occasions of peril—and the one we are recounting is of that number—in which it is necessary to be prodigiously courageous to flee well, to flee with all one's strength and all one's intelligence. Yes, certainly, before the imminence of certain scourges, against which the power of human beings is negligible, it is incontestable that courage must not experience vertigo, must not have a spinning head, must not be soldered or cemented in place by a magnetic torpor, as in a nightmare.

One thing is a great disadvantage to our cavaliers: that is the frequency of wooded and mountainous paths that it is impossible for them to avoid. It is not that access is universally impracticable there, but the asperities of the terrain and the trunks of the trees furnish the serpents with points of support and thrust that they do not encounter on flat ground. Their tails adhere to them, weigh upon them nervously, and they obtain thereby impetus of frightful energy. Thus, several times already, those forming their advance guard have almost come within touching distance of the intrepid fugitives. Already, the warmth of their breath, as torrid as the exhalations of a furnace, has brushed the rumps of the horses.

Charlemagne—who, as we have said, is wearing the costume of an archer—has the corollary bow and arrows. He takes his time and his measures, draws his bow and releases three good arrows one after another, with such fabulous dexterity that he pierces three venomous serpents—the three that are most ardent and in front of the others, which have pressed the horses most closely—and he nails them to the trunks of trees.

That fine exploit, which Libania recompenses with a smile full of eulogies, does not ameliorate the eventualities of the flight; for, instead of intimidating and slowing down the pursuit, it stimulates it and accelerates it further, in the sense that now the reptilian phalanges not only want to punish the sacrilegious theft of their egg but also to avenge the execution of their three leaders.

Look at them! Look at them! Oh, how marvelous it is to go at such a rapid velocity while crawling! It is no longer crawling, it is bounding! It is no longer scraping the dirt, it is cleaving the air. To you, riders! To you, chargers! Force your lungs, muscles and nerves. Take wing. Rival Astolpho and his hippogriff.

I can see that the vigorous chargers are not weakening, that their speed is still the same . . . but it is not sufficient! No, it is not enough that it does not diminish! It is necessary to increase it further, to multiply it tenfold! The great king and the beautiful queen accomplish masterpieces of equitation, which does not prevent them from soon having the breath of the serpents in their backs again.

Suddenly, with a supple and muscular arm, with the promptitude of thought, Charlemagne lifts Libania from her horse and sets her solidly in front of him on his own, against his powerful chest. He is just in time; the maw of a boa has just dug its saw-like teeth into one of the legs of the queen's horse.

Let us not be too alarmed. Let us hope for the flight. That crisis is favorable to it. A relaxation that augurs well results from it. Look! The pursuit, intoxicated by that first success, that first prey, has rushed upon the corpse of the deplorable animal and paused, *en masse*, unanimously. It wallows thereupon joyfully, embracing it with a thousand knots, a thousand meshes. The horse disappears under the profusion, under the density of the coils. The serpents inject their poisons into it, tear it apart joyfully, strip its noble bones, break them and crush them . . .

During that frightful feast, the other horse, with its double burden, gains ground. The two hearts of Charles and Libania are beating in unison with a proud delight—his, for having saved her, hers for having been saved by him. Now that she is clearly edified with regard to the sentiment she has for him, now that her amour is no longer doubtful, she accepts it with a good grace. She abandons herself to it willingly; she will no longer see anything unworthy and reprehensible in it. Emotionally and pensively, she welcomes the promises of happiness that the sentiment whispers to her.

Without speaking, our lovers comprehend one another. Charlemagne has a kind of intimate revelation of Libania's tender thoughts, and his soul is inundated with amorous pride. In his interior triumph, he cries, mentally: *Ha! It's today that I am truly a king!*

However absorbing its action is, that commonality of mysterious contentment still permits our heroes to devote a regretful tear to the generous charger that died so horribly for them. With a spontaneous accord, they dart a glance backwards, as if to honor it with a melancholy adieu.

Oh, it is not over. Look out, my cavaliers! The serpents, having shredded and pulverized their plaything, are not sated. Look out! Now they remember you. Now they are commencing their surge. Now they are running. Here they come! Whatever the distance that you have gained might be, they will soon have caught you up. Your horse is getting weary; it is shedding a stream of sweat over the dust off the paths it is treading. Tremble that it might finally collapse!

Libania gazes at Charles with an energetic despair. She touches the dagger he is carrying in his belt, as if to tell him that its blade is their only recourse . . .

The king extends his hand toward a curtain of willows, ash-trees and bushes that is unfurling on the next horizon, in a hollow in the terrain.

"A river, there!" he tells her, with hope of serenity.

A river! That word enthuses her at first—but she soon reflects that their horse is at great risk of being unable to support the two of them in the midst of the flow, and that they might well die. In any case, death for death, is not that one better than the other?

Meanwhile, the hours have succeeded one another, have accumulated; the daylight is declining; a little more time and it will give way to twilight. Hasten, riders!

They are obliged to go round the sylvan curtain, for it is so thick that it cannot be traversed even on foot, and they start to climb a rather high mound that overlooks the river at the bottom of its far slope.

O desolation! There is no river; it has disappeared; it has run dry. The devouring July sun has drunk three quarters of it. Only a few meager pools of water can still be seen staining its bed of sand and rushes.

Libania raises her eyes to the heavens, and a face sublime with exaltation, and, imitating Clovis at Tolbiac, she cries: "God of Charlemagne, if you deliver us from these monsters, I will embrace you!"[1]

With that, our fugitives, their souls taking refuge in God, pass over the sandy bed to the river.

Now, by an evidently providential hazard, Archbishop Turpin is walking in the vicinity, marching with a placid slowness, reading his breviary and meditating.

He is going to visit one of his friends, a hermit established in the vicinity.

The sound of the running horse disturbs his reading and extracts him from his meditation. He looks . . .

Scarcely has he seen than he comprehends, launches himself forward, and falls to his knees on the bank.

He prays with all his apostolic faith.

God hears him.

At the moment when the reptiles, reaching the other bank, are about to push beyond it, an abundant wave departs, suddenly springing from the furrows of the arid sand, and instead of an almost dry stream, an opulent river appears, which extends, spreads out and caresses its double bank majestically.

---

1 The Frankish king Clovis I is said by legend to have fought the Alamanni at the battle of Tolbiac in 496, although the date is dubious. On the brink of defeat, Clovis is said by Gregory of Tours to have uttered a prayer to the God of his Christian wife Clotilde, including the promise modified by Libania.

Before that insurmountable barrier the serpents recoil. Astonishment brings them down, their thwarted fury crushes them. They suffocate with rage; several of them even die. A few, however, will not admit yet that their defeat is definitive. They climb on to the exuberant branches of the trees on the bank that extend furthest over, wanting to examine whether it might not be possible for them to go from there, with a single leap, to join the branches that present a similar prolongation from the other side of the river. At the first glance they appreciate the enormous difficulty, not to say the impossibility, and, in spite of the exhortation of their fury, they do not hazard the attempt, so apt are those animals always to conserve discernment and prudence in the midst of the most blinding seductions of audacity and hatred. Thus, they abandon the game.

They hasten to quit the theater of their shame. They return as swiftly as they have come.

It would not take much, in the blissful emotion of their deliverance, for Libania and Charlemagne to give one another an expansive and naïve kiss. At least they take hold of one another's hands and shake them enthusiastically. They launch piercing gazes at one another, in which a joyous frenzy is sparkling.

Then, in concert, they divert their sentimental demonstrations toward the saintly archbishop, who is weeping and laughing with satisfaction, and who gives each of them a paternal kiss, like a good friend.

Even the noble charger, by means of an affectionate attitude and a grateful manner, seems to be thanking Monseigneur Turpin for his liberating miracle.

Libania cries, as Corneille's Pauline will one day cry: "I see, I know, I believe! I am disabused! I am a Christian!"

She requests baptism.

Turpin is radiant with glory and happiness. He gladly intones the *Nunc dimittis*.

"Baptism!" he says, ecstatically. "Yes, my child, yes, you shall receive it right away. Look, we'll hold the ceremony over there, in that little chapel you can perceive between two clumps of trees. It is attached to the hermitage of the holy man that I have come to visit, and is served by him. Wait for me here with the King of France. The hermit and I will go to prepare everything."

Charles and Libania, left together, obey the counsel that their lassitude gives them to sit down on the soft grass. It is the second time today that we are seeing them make a station of that sort, but their present disposition is not the one they had the first time. Then, they only understood one another partly; there were still dissonances in the relations of their mutual amour. Charles spoke about his own, if not without hope, at least with animation, so long as it was anxious and veiled. Libania eluded it, defending herself against it, and above all against herself. Now it would be difficult for them to understand one another better. The king speaks of his amour without veils, without apprehension, with a placed wellbeing, in all quietude; and the queen confesses her own with a charming simplicity and purity. They savor the sweetest and finest thing that there is on earth and in heaven: calmness in passion, refreshment in flame.

She tells Charlemagne why the talisman, on which they were relying, was found wanting, and that further proof that he is loved exclusively, although it is superfluous, added to the thousand others that he already has, enchants him sovereignly, and almost brings him to bless the wrath of the monsters.

Their plenitude of joy is so great that, at moments, their speech languishes unfinished, because words fail them—those of human language, that is. That is because they are too far above them; it is because, in ideal amour, there are sanctities that real language does not have the mission to formulate, and relative to which the only means of proving oneself religious is to resign oneself to silence. So, they come to fall completely silent and plunge simultaneously into a delectable meditation.

Oh, how they glorify themselves and congratulate themselves internally, those lovers, since they have nothing to fear from their past, since they are absolute masters of their present, and since they have the wherewithal to make a future for themselves!

Meanwhile, the velvet curtain of evening has descended slowly. The sun has just set. A thin ribbon of pale gold still signals its trace on the mountains and clouds of the Occident. Night and day marry the mystery of their birth and death. Dew falls; perfumes rise. An infinite peace extends its reign over the surroundings. Two divine influences escape from everything and spread everywhere, floating in the air: amour and religion.

Facing our lovers, at a moderate distance, the chapel of the hermitage is situated. The large door has just been opened. The altar, illuminated by numerous candles, stands out splendidly from the broad darkness. That cluster of lights, offered unexpectedly to the eyes of Charles and Libania, imposes devout tremors on them. It seems to them that God is smiling at them in that light, from the depths of the sanctuary. It seems to them that God loves their amour. They imagine that he is present, that he is hovering over them, that he surrounds them and envelops them. They divine him in the nocturnal harmonies that circle them, in the rustle of leaves, in the respiration of soporific winds, in the hum of moths, in the radiance of the stars, in the gleam of fireflies, in the sigh of the nearby water, in the penetrating scents of the grass on which they are reposing. They sense him and see him in everything. Amour is pantheistic.

Turpin emerges from the chapel in sacerdotal costume. Charles and Libania get up and go to meet him. He takes each of them by the arm with a holy and serious gaiety, says a few brief words of paternal unction to them, and takes them with a light, youthful step into the house of God.

There, seconded by the anchorite of the place, he baptizes the Queen of Transylvania with water drawn from the miraculous river.

After the ceremony, Charlemagne leans toward the archbishop's ear. "My good father," he says, in a low and smiling voice, "I beg you to grant Madame and me a second sacrament, immediately. Is there any need to name it?"

The archbishop interrogates Libania with his gaze, and her consent is no less formal for being tacit.

A quarter of an hour later the two lovers have become spouses before God, with no other witnesses than nature, solitude and mystery, all three of which are contemplating them solemnly through all the open doors and windows.

Laugh, bourgeois! Mock my idyllic marriage! At any rate, the witnesses of which I make use, I am proud to say, have no species of relationship with the clownish and indecent crowd that forms corteges for your supposedly virtuous and religious weddings.

The married couple and the archbishop exchange the most touching adieux with the hermit and the hermitage; then all three of them, accompanied by the valorous horse, which Libania mounts alone, set forth to return to the royal residence.

On the way, the good Turpin, who has, naturally, been told the reasons for the quarrel that the serpents had with his friend, says to Charlemagne: "If you deign, dear Sire, to believe the sapience of your old servant, you will decide never to make use of the talisman that you have conquered; you will throw it away or break it. Christ rarely has blessings for the curious arts, for supernatural gifts obtained by ways that are not directly his."

"Are you not too rigid, my friend?" said the king. "The outcome of the adventure justifies the object, it seems to me. Do you know, moreover, that my amour has much to do with this talisman? Considerations of family and politics force me to adjourn for a month the coronation of the queen and the public declaration of our marriage. You can imagine that I cannot resolve to spend all that long time as if I were not Libania's fortunate husband? I do not want her to quit me for a moment; I want to have her incessantly by my side. Now, in order for that to happen without delivering her to the malevolent tongues of calumniators, it is necessary for her to carry on her person the precious egg that will render her invisible to all eyes except mine. Thanks to the egg, we shall escape the serpents of society, just as we have escaped those of creation."

Turpin, who divined without difficulty that Libania was not at all disposed to support him, did not persist.

A fatal condescension, alas!

IV
Love in Death

I F, among the young sons rendered blasé by this age of iron, a few primitive good souls are still led astray by the cult of faerie, the pastoral and knight errantry, and if any of those dear adolescents are numbered among my readers, no doubt the title of this chapter will already have irritated them greatly against me. It is not that I might have put into it a research and affectation that shocks them; oh, their displeasure has a much graver cause. They are holding it against me because I have inscribed a funereal sentence, because I have announced to them that one of my characters—probably my heroine—is going to die, because in that regard I am disappointing them. They have judged, in accordance with the primordial and chivalric mores of my tale that, in order to be logical, it ought to persevere in its series of consoling and cheerful implausibilities; that it ought to "end well," as little children say; that it has an obligation to formulate its conclusion with the sacramental sentence that has always had so much success with naïve and sensitive hearts: "They lived for a long time, were constant and happy, and had an abundant posterity."

And instead of that, instead of showing my spouses in an imperial basilica renewing their fiftieth under the consecrations of the excellent Turpin, I have just offered to separate them prematurely under the condemnation and the reach of inexorable Death, that hideous pontiff who holds a scythe instead of a cross and who produces without modesty to the eyes of the imagination the horrible nudity of her exposed skeleton . . . which is derisory and dolorous!

And yet, young hearts you are wrong to hold it against me; you are wrong to prejudge that I am exempt from paying my espoused lovers the sum of implausible and impossible happiness that is in the rigorous conditions of the genre to which this story belongs. Anyway, will you not admit that mistake benevolently when I have told you that I am only introducing the Sister of Sleep into their midst after having given them a whole month of true, perfect happiness? Yes, an entire month, a frank, complete, integral month! Thirty days and thirty nights of terrestrial paradise!

Do not pretend, children, that that is very little, that I am showing an ill grace in protesting so much, and that the dose of happiness in question is not outside the scope of the possible. Interrogate people who live more in the soul and the mind than the body, who are both people of passion and understanding They will tell you that the practitioners of veritable and durable amour who have the least complaint to make against fate, those whose romance is the least traversed, never possess a month of continuous happiness, and that if all the happy hours disseminated in the long period of their passion—a passion that often occupies two thirds of their life, in the final count—were detached and reunited it is probably that there would not even be enough of them to constitute the value of a month.

At that statement, I believe I can hear the zealots of Hymen mocking my peremptory tone and inviting me to recognize that my assertion only applies to illegitimate amour, that it cannot in any fashion concern marriage, and that I am not making an extraordinary gift to my characters by granting them an entire month of amorous wellbeing, in view of the fact that the first month of any conjugal union has the privilege of being an irreproachable specimen of bliss, as the "wisdom of nations" testifies by granting it the symbolic title of "honeymoon."

In truth, Messieurs the orthodox, I am scarcely able, being an unworthy bachelor, to treat *ex cathedra* the strength and weakness of that famous "moon." However, I dare to remind you that the aforementioned wisdom of nations is an arrant hypocrite, which often amuses itself by contradicting quietly what it says aloud. For instance, you might have heard it insinuated slyly that the moon of honey is always followed by the moon of bile,[1] and afterwards, that the latter is not content to succeed her elder sister immediately, and always curtails somewhat the former's reign, that it is not for want of putting horns on her, and that sometimes it does not even permit her to be born, preceding her above the matrimonial horizon . . .

---

1 The phonetic wordplay linking *lune de miel* [honeymoon] with *lune de fiel* [moon of bile] does not translate, alas, and English usage only rarely credits a crescent moon with having "horns," thus not really facilitating sly references to cuckoldry.

I suspect, my reverends, that the wordplay that rhymes *miel* and *fiel* inspires you and causes you umbrage. Let's see, will you not push injustice and ill-humor to the point of accusing me of heresy? To the point of reproaching me for swelling the infamous host who blaspheme marriage and want to demolish it?

Who, me? Me, pass for a blasphemer and a demolisher of that holy institution? Oh, it is with my forehead in the dust that I protest my reverence, my respect and my veneration for it! On approaching its region I am subject to the sacred terror to which people were subject in antiquity as they approached the vicinity of the lair of Trophonius! And it is not only my instinctive and affective faculties that render that homage; it is also the forces of my intelligence, my thought and my reason! Marriage! But every thinker, every reasoner, ought to adhere to it! Marriage, God's truth, is the vertebral column of the social body. It is more than a holy thing, it is a necessary thing, and it has an importance equal to the law of recruitment to military discipline, to the magistracy, to the gendarmerie, to the National Guard.

Oho! I detect around me a whisper of disapproval. Are people taxing as satirical my honest comparisons? Decidedly, I can see that I am dealing with prejudiced judges. I am flattering myself in vain that I might persuade them that I am not guilty. That is why I shall take refuge in the divinity of my mantle, and resume my task of an innocent storyteller.

So, my Libania and my Charlemagne were the possessors for a full month of the felicity of an amour without mixture and without measure. I shall not undertake to describe and analyze it. It has been observed that the ideal of amour is far more inaccessible to the brushes of human expression than the ideal of dolor; and that impotence is no less the share of geniuses of the first order than secondary minds. Dante and Milton, so sublime with force and color when they paint the terrors and the tortures of the Inferno, show themselves to be feeble and dull when they try to paint the splendors and delights of Paradise.

The day after the last day of our luminous month, the Queen of Transylvania received when she awoke a message from the prime minister of her realm, who told her that her subjects had just revolted, proclaimed her fall and elected in her place one of the former pretenders to the throne.

That news caused her chagrin but did not astonish her, for she knew full well that the influence of her ring could only act on one person alone since her exclusive and special amour for a single person.

She went to tell Charlemagne about the event. In order to dissipate her chagrin, he said: "Your property will soon be returned to you, my love. Have no fear. We will go to take it back ourselves at the head of a respectable army. We will punish these rebels with the efficacious energy that I have put so many times into the punishment of the Saxons."

Those reprisals and implacable vengeances were scarcely to the taste of the merciful Libania, who had set, as we know, such beautiful precedents in the matter of political abnegation, so she replied:

"My knight mistakes the nature of the displeasure I'm experiencing. It isn't the loss of the kingdom that saddens me. What does Transylvania matter to me, who will be crowned Queen of France in three days and designated to the homage of nations as the legitimate and beloved wife of Charlemagne? What is painful to me is simply the ingratitude of the people I loved, whose wellbeing I had commenced and hoped to continue. But I beg you, no war against them. Let them govern themselves as they wish. Perhaps their new choice is good. The man who replaces me might be worth as much."

"Worth as much as you, flame of the Orient!" cried the king, transported. "God might have a twin sister and she could scarcely be worth as much as you! But you have ideas regarding the art of government, my friend, that my experience forbids me to admit. I tell you that I am very resolved to punish these ingrates. Don't make any objection; we'll talk about this again later. I'll try to enable you to adopt speculations less sublime, it's true, but more practicable. It's necessary not to treat the affairs of human beings superhumanly; it's necessary to keep them close at hand and underfoot, and not to let them covet from on high what lies beneath. In any case, console yourself. My Franks, whom you will soon command, are as generous and faithful as their name. Their gratitude, which is assured to you in advance for all the happiness with which you cannot fail to heap them, will aid you gently to forget the ingratitude of those barbarians, who truly merit taking back, not to quit it again, their original name of Avars."

"Your words always delight me, my sweet lord," said Libania. "Nevertheless, no matter how I deliver myself to their charm, I cannot help seeing this revolt as a bad augury. It is rare that a calamity comes alone. Misfortune so easily engenders misfortune. My God, my God, what will become of me now? My amour is afraid."

"Nothing can happen to us but fortunate things, my white fay," said Charles, with a smiling firmness, "nothing that is not linked and bound to our present destiny. There is only one misfortune of amour that ought to frighten amour. Come on, let us not think any more about your culpable realm. Forget those who have forgotten you. Occupy your mind cheerfully. Look, brilliant military games are going to take place in an hour on the palace esplanade. Watch them. That kind of amusement has always pleased you. Having the intention to figure in them myself, I have a double reason for desiring you to be a spectator. Equip yourself, therefore, with the egg of invisibility and mount the platform of the southern tower. You will have a marvelous view from there to admire your knight's fine thrusts of the lance. You can float above us, invisible and mysterious, as befits a fay, or an angel."

Libania went up on to the tower. The warrior fête commenced. People of imagination who are reading me, reawaken all the poetic memories of readings that you have made in the blue library.[1] Recall all that you

---

1 The *bibliothèque bleue* [blue library] was the name given to a species of popular pamphlet which began publication is the early seventeenth century and did not die away completely until the early nineteenth. The pioneering specimens produced by Jean and Nicolas Oudot had blue paper covers. It featured, among many other things, digests of numerous Medieval romances, rendering those originally published in verse into prose, and helped enormously to popularize their substance.

have seen there of passes of arms, tourneys, jousts and carousels, and have the kindness to imagine that all the merits scattered in those different acts of fine warfare are assembled and concentrated in the one that is unfolding at the feet of my heroine. That kindness of your part will spare both of us a task: me the labor of a description, and you the tedium of reading it, or at least the simple tedium of skipping over a few lines. You will, in consequence, admit summarily that Charlemagne executes feats in which the strength of Renaud, the skill of Roland and the elegance of Olivier are found in combination: both the straightforward impetuosity of the Northern knights and the supple muscularity of the southern knights.

Libania is entirely abandoned to the thousand prestiges of his splendor. She is no longer conscious of anything else. The impression of the morning's disgraceful news has vanished. Her mind, her thoughts, her heart and her soul no longer have any other concern than gazing and ecstasizing.

Meanwhile, the men-at-arms armored in iron are succeeded by lightly-armed jousters: arbalestiers, pliers of quarterstaffs and archers. The last-named are particularly prodigious. Their arrows fly into the depths of the sky to seek out eagles and merlins almost imperceptible to the eye, so high are they flying, and those birds of prey fall into the arena struck by death.

One of them, however, is less afflicted than the others. It retains sufficient vigor to stop on the way down and to come and settle on one of the crenellatons of the tower on which Libania is standing. The archer who has fired at it, furious and ashamed at only having wounded it, unleashes a new arrow . . .

But the hand of the bowman, whose anger causes it to tremble, lacks dexterity for a second time. The arrow deviates, and, instead of hitting the bird, plunges, alas into Libania's breast.

She utters a horrible scream.

Shrill and penetrating as that cry is, it is so drowned out by the mocking jeers that the archer's awkwardness has excited that it is not heard by anyone—except Charlemagne. For that voice, the appeal of distress of that voice, he would have heard through the din of a world collapsing.

He launches forth, runs and disappears from the tourney; and his disappearance is scarcely noticed at first so enormous are the racket and the disorder. But soon, the words: "The king is no longer there!" have circulated from mouth to mouth and have gradually appeased the tumult. A semi-silence is established. People look around; they interrogate one another in low voices.

They see, in the grounds of the palace, a great movement of pages and lords. Gradually, the rumor spreads that the Queen of Transylvania, attacked by a sudden illness, is on a bed of dolor, that she is dying, and that the king and the archbishop are alone with her. And, in accordance with the eternal custom of social tongues, the cause of that accident, which no one yet knows, is altered and denatured in the accounts. It is said, against any appearance of truth, that it is the king who has stabbed the princess himself, in a transport of furious jealousy.

Alas, it is only the insulting part of those rumors that is untrue. The rest is only too real. Yes, indeed, Libania is dying. Already, her beautiful body is impregnated with the icy moisture of death. Old Turpin, who is very knowledgeable in the healing art, has said, shaking his head, after a long examination of the wound: "Sire, human knowledge can do nothing here."

Charles, beside himself with desolation, is leaning over his beloved. His amour is trying desperately to dispute her with death.

His eyes and his breath cover her, trying to warm her again; all his energy, all his soul, all his thought, all his palpitation, all the moral and vital strength with which he is overflowing, which extend over her, inundating her, are endeavoring to transfuse her profusely with their vigor and their flame. Three times, their action has appeared to triumph. Three times, Libania has smiled, has shuddered, as if reanimated, as if grasping existence again . . . but three times, also, she has fallen back, pale, bloodless and moribund. She senses clearly that all is lost, and she makes a sign to Charles to place his ear very close to her lips.

"Enough, friend," she says to him. "Don't torment destiny. Even the breath of our amour is impotent against the breath of Death. Her profound darkness is drawing me; I'm descending into it; I'm falling . . . My soul, which is not falling, which is, on the contrary, rising higher in order to continue its immortality there . . . what is my soul going to do, what is it going to do without you? Without you, how can I be happy in Heaven? And you who remain, what will you do after me? Oh, the idea that perhaps, one day, another woman . . . that cruel, that frightful idea tears me apart, kills me far more than the wound from which I'm dying . . . ! Shut up, shut up. Don't say anything. Don't protest. Don't swear. I'm wrong, I know it, I accuse myself of it. You will never love anyone but me. Pardon my jealousy. No, I have no need of a solemn oath to be tranquil. Look, I only ask one thing. Promise me to leave this ring on my finger, and to make sure that no one comes to take it away from me. Promise me that!"

The lover promises with all his passion, amid a deluge of tears, sobs and words intercut by kisses of adieu.

The forehead of the dying lover illuminates slightly . . . she throws one last spark into her gaze—and she dies.

When Charles can no longer doubt his disaster, when he has fully experimented that none of his amour can make the soul that has flown away descend again, he kneels, haggard, against the mortuary bed, and is immobilized for a few moments in mute contemplation before the beautiful corpse still clad in her festival costume. Then he stands up and, trembling with delirium, seizing his royal mantle from a nearby armchair where it is lying unfurled, he covers his mistress with it, gently, wrapping her in it with tender precaution. Then he picks her up, thus enveloped, poses her with piety in his robust arms, and leaves the room, carrying her through a secret passage, after having made a sign to Turpin, the only other person present, not to follow him.

From that fatal day onwards, the king applies himself to fleeing the society of humans, even that of his dearest friends. He scarcely appears in his ordinary apartments for an hour a day in order to give audience there to his ministers and generals. The rest of the time he remains enclosed in the most august of the profundities of his palace, in a magical habitation, a *sanctum sanctorum* that had made the delights of Libania, where he had spent sublime moments with her, and to which the queen, in her recognition, had taken pleasure in giving the sweet name of the *Sélam.*[1] She and he excepted, no other human being, not even his friend the archbishop, has ever penetrated there. They would have attempted to do so in vain, moreover, for the abode was constructed in such a manner that the door could not be found without the instructions of the architect. It was the enchanter Maugis who had built it, with the sole aid of his art, and it was said that invisible genii served the king there.

A number of days and weeks passed thus. Although the affairs of the realm did not suffer from the voluntary sequestration of the king, who ruled it as skillfully as before from the depths of his retreat, the sage Turpin nevertheless conceived great anxieties and urgent alarms concerning the temporal reason and the eternal salvation of Charles. What motivated such apprehensions above all was that several times after asking his master why he did not proceed with the funeral of the dead woman, he had never obtained any other response than a gaze full of anger, which commanded silence in a terrible fashion.

For the good of his royal friend, he resolved to look into the mystery. With that objective he went to find the enchanter, confided his design to him, explained his motives, and summoned him, in the name of Jesus Christ, to procure him the means of putting it into execution. Maugis was very devout in spite of being given to the

______

1 i.e., the ceremonial greeting sometimes rendered *salaam* in English usage, derived from the Arabic word for peace.

occult science, for God he violated the oath that he had given the king. The prelate received all the necessary instructions from him, and, thanks to them, introduced himself furtively into the Sélam during the hour when the king's habitude abstained from it.

The Sélam was an exceedingly singular place. Its multiple essence participated in the labyrinth of Crete, the subterrains of Persepolis, Druidic temples and Moorish alcazars. When Turpin had negotiated an infinity of narrow corridors filled with deceptive curves and misleading entrances and exists, he reached a vast and ostentatious chamber, curiously ornamented.

It was ovoid in form—the most sacred form after that of the delta. On each side it had seven windows cut into trefoils, which opened over woods of aloes and fields of lilies, where brilliant and harmonious water played in granite fountains. Fabrics of an impossible richness, sustained by clasps of fabulous diamonds, draped its walls. Paintings representing the principal amorous scenes of the *Song of Songs* decorated its ceilings. In the indentations and the intervals between the windows, on the entablature and the moldings of the door, and then again in vases, baskets and tripods, an immense quantity of flowers was grouped, arranged and spread, which seemed freshly picked, and over the organization of which a taste had presided that was full of caprice, and nevertheless of grandeur.

The interest produced by those generalities of ornamentation were quickly effaced, however, before that engendered by a particular and unique marvel, exposed uniquely and specially at the back of the room on a magnificent platform. That platform, gold and silver, silk and velvet, was surmounted by a similar dais, under which stood a seat that was not a throne and not a bed but a kind of compromise between the two. On the cushions of that royal seat reposed a woman, and that woman was Libania, a corpse.

At the sight of her the good archbishop experienced a great tenderness. The noble old man was far from having lost the memory of the sage pleasures of amity that had united him with her. Above all, he was far from having forgotten the solemn joy he had had in making her a Christian.

She was still beautiful. None of the alterations that result from death were visible in her. She only had the pallor and immobility of the tomb. Although she had been dead for several months, she still conserved the whiteness and the freshness that she had possessed on the day of her sudden death. She had the same beauty, and was clad in the same garments. Over her parted lips and in her half-closed eyes, a certain vague reminiscence of her last smile still floated. In the abandoned attitude of her limbs something still remained of her firm and sinewy grace; she had nothing, or almost nothing, of heavy inertia, of the flaccid stuffiness and the softness if the articulations customary in corpses. Certainly, it was not life, but it was not entirely death. It was the beauty of the former grafted on to the impassivity of the latter.

Arcanum of arcana! Prodigy of prodigies! Duality no less terrible than charming! Simultaneity of fear and delight . . .

Turpin, who knew how well Maugis was versed in the science of spells, hesitated nevertheless to believe that he was sufficiently so to have been able to extract without auxiliary aid such a concession from the jealous despotism of trespass. To blunt the needle of death! He estimated that such a miracle could only have been made with the aid of a talisman come from the Orient, that central hearth of the marvelous, that metropolis of magic. He remembered then that Libania had been born and brought up in Persia, the land of Zoroaster: a reflection that led him also to remember the recommendation that she had made Charlemagne at the moment of her death to leave her ring on her finger and to make certain that no one removed it. He told himself that the agent of the miracle must be that mysterious ring.

A sound of footsteps drew him out of that preoccupation. Swiftly, he hid behind a curtain.

Charlemagne came in with an impetuous passion, but as soon as he crossed the threshold it was as if he were gripped by recollection and his march slowed by degrees, He was sumptuously dressed and perfumed, like a gallant cavalier going to an amorous rendezvous. He was almost as pale as the dead darling at whom his intense gaze was directed. A touching mixture of masculine and profound tenderness, funereal melancholy and exalted religion characterized his entire person. He held his right hand, tightly clenched and pressed against his breast, as if he needed to repress pulsations that were too violent and an excessive swelling. In fact, the precipitate and jerky murmur of his respiration announced that an ardent blood was flowing from his heart.

He threw himself rather than knelt beside his pale beloved; there he was more at ease, he breathed better; there he could release and pour out the seraphic effluvia of his strange amour. It overflowed in idolatrous words and fervent tears. It dissolved in caresses of soul and flame that were not, it can certainly be presumed, incompatible with the sanctity and majesty of death.

As one does to a favorite child, he kissed the beautiful naked feet of the queen: her beautiful little feet, adorable in vigor and finesse. He disturbed and rearranged the pleats of her dress, varying its capricious elegances at his pleasure. He undid and rearranged her long and opulent black hair; he paraded his lips over its silky tresses, plunged his face recklessly into its waves, extended them like a veil and put them up like a diadem. Without precisely displacing her body, without altering the harmonious ensemble of its pose, he changed it, modifying its accidents, and at each of those modifications, each of those changes, he paused and smiled gloriously, as if to declare—which was true—that there did not exist a single aspect under which the omnipotence of her charm could seem diminished.

Then, parting his lover's bodice with a trembling finger, he considered with a chaste despair the wound that had caused her death. That fatal wound was still fresh and crimson, although blood was no longer flowing from it. He placed his pious mouth upon it gently, lightly, and sowed thousands of kisses there, accompanied by an incessant dew of tears.

Then he called his lover by the sweetest appellations, inventing divine nomenclatures in order to name her.

He evoked their beautiful amorous past, he enumerated and saluted its fortunate raptures. He regretted at length, in the bitterness in which his heart was floating, that of those days and nights of gold and honey there did not subsist, at least, a living and visible emanation, a work, a symbol, a trophy: which is to say, a child . . .

Then he took possession of the hand on which the magic ring was shining, and endowed that hand with his best kisses, covering the ring with them, above all.

Gradually, those passionate manifestations calmed down, to give way to another genre of delirium, seemingly less disorderly, but in reality even more bizarre.

He stood up, went to take a few tomes and a sheet of parchment from a nearby credenza, and then came back to take his place very close to Libania, no longer kneeling madly and frenetically, no longer in an eccentric attitude, no longer with a grave stance, but sitting normally. He opened several of the books in turn, which had all belonged to the queen and had been honored by her preference, and he read aloud various fragments of chivalric stories, poems and theological dissertations. He read with verve and eloquence, and from time to time he interrupted his reading to study his lover's features. The victim of an enchanting illusion, he imagined that he glimpsed furtive marks of jubilation there, and, transported by joy, he resumed and continued with an increase of verve and pleasure.

When he had finished those readings he deployed the parchment and wrote thereon, in a rapid and firm hand, a page that he also read aloud. It was a political explanation treating the current affairs of the realm. This time, he was not content to look at Libania in order to know her opinion; he leaned over her and applied his ear to her mouth. He remained thus for some time, imagining that he could hear something—after which he took up his page again, reread it, still aloud, and made corrections in accordance with the observations that he was persuaded that he had heard.

Afterwards, he lay down languidly and somberly at the feet of his mistress, and, with multiple sighs, he fell profoundly sleep.

To those whom the profundity of that sleep might astonish, I will say that sleeping well is the prerogative of two kinds of people: people whose are excellently happy and people who are utterly unhappy. Is it not hope that generally occasions insomnia? When one no longer hopes for anything, either because one has reached the summit of happiness or because one is lying in the ultimate pit of despair, one sleeps fully with a flavorsome lethargy. On the night that followed immediately the defeat and fall of Waterloo, Napoléon slept like a sepulchral statue. During the night that succeeded the day on which she believed herself certain of being loved by Louis XIV as much as she loved him, Madame de La Vallière enjoyed an immensely calm and serene repose, like a pure lake radiantly somnolent under the summer sun.[1]

Charles slept with an intensity all the greater because he united within himself those two conditions of extreme unhappiness and extreme happiness: extreme unhappi-

---

1 Louise de La Baume Le Blanc did not become the Duchesse de La Vallière until she was no longer the king's mistress, but is always remembered by that name.

ness in knowing full well that Death would not release her prey; extreme happiness in having the intimate persuasion that the lifeless body was nevertheless not devoid of amour, in thinking that the non-alteration of her admirable beauty was the great work of that amour, which had survived death.

As soon as he recognizes the plenitude of that slumber, Turpin slowly abandons his retreat and advances at a mute pace toward the two lovers.

What is he going to do? What is his intention? Are you going to tell me, my very young and very good readers? Will he have the courage, the cruelty, to want . . . ?

Alas, yes. That's it. He wants to remove the ring in order to break the charm.

Certainly, it has cost him to resolve to strike such a blow, being as he is so indulgent, and so sensitive. It is not without great interior torments that he is determined to deprive that poor dead woman and his faithful friend of their mysterious consolations. But his austere theologian's conscience recommends him to do it. It makes him believe that it is necessary, indispensable to the salvation of the king's soul. That cult of amour, that exclusive devotion to the deceased beauty, although there is nobility and purity in them, seem to Turpin to constitute a deadly idolatry capable of conducting Charles to eternal damnation.

Ha! Theologians of all theologies, you are all like that. You have no pity, no mercy for the hiccups of the feeble human heart. You break them barbarously under the pretext of pleasing God, the universal God, the true God, whose indulgence is as infinite as his excellence, who is all peace and all mercy. You do that even when you have guts, even when you have not forgotten that you are born of woman. The intoxication of dictatorship carries you away involuntarily, I would like to think. Do you have the right to establish yourself thus as agents of the Divinity's affairs and to model those affairs in the fashion of Humanity—which is to say, to suppose in God our passions, our exigencies and our hatreds? Dare you adjoin to the sublime substantive *God* the wretched adjectives *angry* and *jealous*? Is it a wise judgment to give a divine reign the corollary of a human government? Is there justice and rectitude in regulating the relationship between God and humankind in accordance with the relationships between human beings?

I can hear you responding that these things have been said and repeated a hundred times over, or their equivalent, in the eighteenth century. Well, perhaps it is not inappropriate to repeat them in the nineteenth, for they are good things. I am not unaware that your scribes, with the tips of their disdainful pens, willingly qualify that as bad taste, as bad manners. Good, provided that it is not bad logic.

Turpin has arrived next to Libania. He takes her hand and lifts it, tremulously. He cannot hold back a large tear, which falls slowly and heavily on to that hand. Nevertheless, his resolution does not weaken. He gets ready to steal the ring . . .

Charlemagne, fortunately and unfortunately at the same time—continues to slumber with amplitude, not having the appearance of thinking of waking up: fortunately, because if a sudden awakening presented him with the archbishop carrying out his larceny, he would doubtless commit a crime, would doubtless stab his faithful and beloved companion to death; unfortunately, because he is about to be dispossessed of his miraculous joys, his dear dove and his love-nest, so strangely nestled in the tree of death.

The ring is removed . . .

At that instant, a deplorable transformation is accomplished in the dead woman and everything surrounding her.

Over that charming body, so fresh and so harmonious, a little flickering flame passes rapidly back and forth, which takes away its freshness and its harmony, which changes it into a mummified body, with desiccated flesh, parchmented, green and bistre, its fibers elongated and as rigid as a sheaf of spears. Funerary bandages have replaced its adornments.

The gold and silver, silk and velvet of the seat and the platform are metamorphosed into bronze and black marble. The rich drapes of the chamber have fallen into dust and have given way to the rugged nudity of the wall of a catacomb. All the flowers in the garlands and the baskets have withered suddenly, and a glacial wind, launched from all the windows, whirls their pale debris.

Externally, the metamorphosis is as complete. The brilliant and profound blue sky has become low and dull. The wood of myrtles and aloes is no longer anything but a cypress wood. The clumps of lilies and irises are no longer anything but bushes of marigolds and poppies; the pure fountains are stagnant and troubled pools.

Now, it is entirely a sepulcher, all is darkness—*darkness visible*, as the English Homer says, so terribly—all is death.

Charles has woken with a start; he is on his feet; he looks around fearfully. He cannot believe his eyes! He tells himself, full of conviction, that it is a dream; he wonders, astonished, how such a dream has dared to trouble with its horrors the chastely amorous slumber that he savors in the atmosphere of his lover's melancholy beauty. Delivered to the belief that he is still asleep, he makes a thousand efforts to wake up . . .

It does not take him long to recognize that he has nothing to do for that. The truth, the frightful truth, presses him, covers him, invades him, and renders him mad with grief.

Finally, he perceives the archbishop, who is smiling to him with an entirely evangelical sadness and amity, who is holding out his sexagenarian arms to him. He precipitates himself into them effusively.

"My father, my father!" he cries, sobbing. "Oh, pity me, weep with me. How apt it is that you are here! My heart is broken, crushed! You can have no suspicion of what I have lost! A splendid, adorable, ineffable illusion, which had such gripping characteristics of reality that I scarcely dare call it illusion! I would far rather endure the loss of my kingdom! How much less the pain would be! My father, my father, it's horrible! You see, it's as if my Libania had died a second time. Listen and judge."

And, agitated by an immense regret, moved by the most tender passion, he recounts the bizarre things that we have just revealed.

Turpin weeps warm tears with him, flatters his despair, taking a share of it, tells him and repeats to him that he will not try to console him, that it is impossible . . . which is the best manner of consolation.

The king emerges gradually from the excess of his agitation, embraces his friend again, and says to him: "My good Turpin, I recall that, throughout the duration of that illusion, so dear and so regrettable, you insinuated to me several times that it was my duty to proceed with the funeral ceremony. I offended you then with a taciturn and haughty refusal. That offense you will easily pardon in view of my blind folly. Now that my reason is no longer enslaved, you see me ready to fulfill the sacred duty that I rejected when it was. But we shall conduct the ceremony without pomp, without publicity, in the darkness, just the two of us. I desire that the jealous mystery that presided over my Libania's marriage and brief royalty should also preside over her funeral. I want the secret to remain between us. Will you please, then, my father, go in search of everything necessary to celebrate a black mass. You will be the officiant and I the servant."

Turpin, who, as we have seen, had the gift of miracles, detached his pastoral cross from his breast and made use of it to trace a triangle on the ground at the foot of the queen's monument.

Suddenly, an altar emerged from the ground at that place: a funereal altar, with its luminary and its black drapery edged with white. The divine sacrifice was celebrated.

In spite of his true and profound trouble, the officiant maintained until the end a worthily impassive air and countenance, as was appropriate to his ministry. It was not the same for the servant; several times, he suddenly dissolved in tears, launched himself toward the body of the queen, threw himself upon it, seized it and clasped it, exhaling heat-rending lamentations.

But the poor dead woman could not rejoice in or be proud of those embraces; they differed too much from those she had received before her ring had been stolen. There was still a fervent veneration, but there was no longer the holy fury of possession She was no longer embraced as something that was, but as something that had been. That tenderness no longer honored her body as a being loved in person, but simply the vestment deprived of the beloved being.

Those symptoms, which did not escape the archbishop, satisfied him by proving to him that the final reflections of the king's bewitchment were fading away. He assisted that by elevating Charles's interior gaze toward Paradise, signaling to him in the celestial life the immortal soul of Libania, which was waiting for him, and would not suffer in waiting. He profited sagely from the salutary, soporific reverie into which that prospect of immortality plunged him in order to draw him, by means of a gentle and gradual effort, out of the lugubrious Sélam.

Libania's body remained free and uncovered on the beautiful table of bronze and black marble. Charles did not want it to be imprisoned, nor nailed into a coffin. His mind had the conviction that everything was really finished, but he had in his sensitive flesh some rebellious instinct to persuade him that the insensible flesh of the woman he had adored ought not to suffer such a narrow confinement and such an absolute deprivation of air.

Those who have worn mourning for a cherished person will understand that bizarre instinct, that singular reluctance.

Furthermore, the queen's cadaver could do without a bier, without any consequential deterioration since, having been, as we have seen, reduced to the state it was in, it was exempt from decomposition—let us not mince words—from putrefaction.

Whatever decay had been inflicted on her by the theft of her ring, the flame of purification that had run over her entire body at the moment when it came under the common law again was not a scornful adieu on the part of that talisman. That supernatural embalming was not a mediocre conclusion to her privileged destiny; for the most terrible hideousness of death consists a thousand times less in the alteration of the features and the deterioration of the contours than in the repulsive fermentation and frightful deterioration of the human substance.

What horror there is in knowing that a beloved corpse dissolves gradually into filthy matter like a vile animal, falling into a similar putrescence; in thinking, alas, that the angelic body on an idolized child, the sacred body of a cherished mother, the precious body of a noble lover, is subject in the tomb to an abominable ruination, the perception of which would strike with an invincible disgust the devoted father, the pious son, the exalted lover . . .

Oh, how enviable antiquity is, therefore, for its worthy and holy custom of incinerating the dead!

✳

On one of the following nights, the archbishop saw the queen in a dream. She was resplendent with bliss, but nevertheless, she had a nuance of melancholy in her visage; a hint of shadow attenuated the light of her pure forehead.

She told him mildly that he was mistaken, that the effects of the ring had nothing blameworthy, that Charles's salvation had never been compromised by it. She advised him, in terms and with a smile of perfect benevolence, no longer to be so prompt in establishing himself as the appreciator of the will of the Almighty without his preliminary advice.

When he awoke, Turpin was initially somewhat troubled, involuntarily, by that vision. He even had a commencement of remorse. But he soon steeled himself by telling himself, in a trenchant and deliberate fashion, that the dream could not be veridical and that it might well have been an insinuation of the Evil One.

In truth, I know of nothing comparable to the obstinacy of theologians—except that of philosophers.

It only remains for me to inform the world of what became of the ring.[1] That will be the subject of a final chapter.

---

1 The reader might think that it also remains for him to say what happened to the Serpents' Egg, which appears to have been completely forgotten.

V

The Temptation of the Archbishop

ANOTHER title that is of a nature to stimulate discontentments and incriminations! "An archbishop in temptation—what a scandal!" certain reactors of ultramontanism might cry. "But that is an impious spectacle a sacrilegious invention! Oh, unfortunate poet, you are too much the son of this blasphemous and incredulous century, which compensates itself for not being able to persecute the Church, the immaculate spouse of the Messiah, physically by persecuting it morally with the examining pride and insidious reasoning of Julian the Apostate!"[1]

Truly, yes, it is not impossible that such a warning, no less banal and solemn, might be cried upon my humble storyteller's fantasy. For our so-called enlightened epoch is swarming with austere personages superlatively inclined to wax umbrageous and indignant, every time that the

---

1 In reading passages such as this, it is worth recalling that the story was originally published as a serial in a right-wing newspaper, *La Patrie*, where its episodes might well have called forth such voluble ripostes, which would have been communicated to the writer while he was still in the process of composing his story.

imagination of a writer, in a novel, a poem or a drama, placing on stage a member of the priesthood, represents him as a mere mortal, the object of the solicitations and weaknesses of this world. And note well that that virtuous wrath, that honest indignation, does not arise uniquely when the priest succumbs, when the terrestrial element has the upper hand, which might at least excuse them; they arise even when the priest emerges from the struggle victorious, when the fact of his story is a splendid homage rendered to the efficacy of the Christian faith!

And let me not be accused of recriminating falsely. To prove that what I am saying is strictly true and that I am not exaggerating, I could quote a thousand eloquent examples. I will only cite one that is typical of them all, which was placing Lamartine's *Jocelyn* on the Index.[1] Is that comprehensible? Jocelyn, that Catholic masterpiece, criticized and condemned by the Holy See! All of you who have read it and reread it, do you know anything that has edified you more than that book, which has made you want more to become a believer again? What is better made to bring into the light the omnipotence of Christianity with regard to our passions, even in regard to those that have grandeur and purity, than that admirable story, in which a modest country curé, with the sole assistance of divine religion, puts an end, without enduring the slightest fall, to an amour all the more difficult to tame because it is almost divine itself?

They are funny people, messieurs the clergy, to take exception, and claim to be insulted because they are de-

---

1 Alphonse de Lamartine's long poem *Jocelyn* was first published in 1836.

clared to be susceptible, I do not say to sin, but simply to temptation—people who comment on the gospel, in which the Savior himself is seen to resign himself, as the Son of Man, to being tempted by the Devil!

Meanwhile, friend Turpin, who has put the magic ring on his finger, receives incomparable benefits from it. The affection and consideration that the king and the kingdom have testified to him for such a long time, have been increased immeasurably. In the Church and in the army, in the administration and in the arts, nothing is done that has not been passed by his approval—what am I saying? which has not been proposed and advised by him. Henceforth, the veritable arbiter of peace and war is him No envy or criticism hampers him. Public opinion at every level and every rank is exclusively affectionate to him. His omnipotent favor next to the throne is accepted by everyone as the most natural and most necessary thing in the world. The king keeps him by his side incessantly; he will not suffer being distanced from him for a moment. He makes him sleep in his own chamber, under his own tent.

Charlemagne believes that he can explain and justify this redoubling of favor and sympathy by means of the reflection that the archbishop is the only person initiated into the secret of his love for Libania, the only one who has known all the merits of that adored woman. At every moment of the day he talks to him about her; by night he wakes him up in order to talk to him about her again.

In the meantime, the Gauls have become embroiled in a new war with Germany. The theater of hostilities is the land of the Belgians, a country that the future will habituated to serving as a theater for that kind of drama. Charlemagne has pitched his camp there.

It is night. The tents and their avenues are finally silent. Everyone is asleep except for the sentinels and the patrols . . . and also our friend Archbishop Turpin. That is not, however, because Charlemagne, in whose tent his bed is located, is raising the slightest obstacle to his repose or retaining him in the slightest conversation. No, Charlemagne is profoundly asleep. What is preventing Turpin from sleeping is the rivalry of two thoughts, which are contending in his mind, two powerful opposites that are agitating in his soul and disputing it. He is trying in vain to dominate that tumult and impose silence on it, trying in vain to adjourn the settlement of that moral duel, trying in vain to soothe his agitated imagination, exhorting himself in vain to go to sleep. The antagonism of his heart will not grant him any truce. He has solicited one, harassed to a point that proves to him that it wants to constrain him to a definitive option without letting go.

He escapes feverishly from his bed, which is burning him. He emerges from the tent, which is weighing upon him; his lungs need air, his entire body needs movement and space.

He goes back and forth, striding through the peaceful streets of the camp. But here again he feels confined. The proximity of people inconveniences and obfuscates him; he needs solitude. Thus, he goes forth, he walks on and on, until he is outside the lines of the camp, until he has left them far behind him.

He stops on the edge of a small diaphanous lake, framed on the horizon by a hemicycle of wooded mountains. The night is beautiful, a warm August night. The stars of the heavens are reproduced admirably by the mirror of the motionless liquid—so admirably that the gaze, by virtue of contemplating the water and the sky, might reach the point of no longer knowing which of them is the mirror of the other.

That great luxury of calm and serenity has no effect on the stormy dreamer. His intimate duel continues, no less furiously.

But what is its subject?

This: in substance, in summary, this is the language with which, without repose, since sunset, the two voices of ardent thoughts, have been disputing his will; these, in their clearest expression, are the two themes that they never cease to develop, to paraphrase, exhausting their oratory resources competitively:

"Consider," says the first voice, "that it can be effectuated without inflicting the slightest damage on anyone, that it will even be joy and wellbeing of many. Does the seductive power of the ring have limits? No, the king, as soon as you speak to him about it, will throw his arms around you and concede enthusiastically his abdication in your favor, apologizing for not having divined your desire, which he ought to have foreseen. The unanimous adhesion of the people will follow passionately that of the king. The crown will be well and truly on your venerable head

"It is already you who governs; your influence is everything; it is just and reasonable that it is you who reigns. You need the title and the insignia of the command that you exercise. In appropriating them, it is not a carnal and reprehensible desire that you are satisfying; your character has nothing in common with what is base; the noble and praiseworthy ambition that dominates you exclusively is that of rendering the human race better and happier. You can work from then on in a more direct and more immediate fashion in putting your magnanimous ideas to work. Your science and your bounty are superior to Charlemagne's, whose warrior life has sometimes hardened his heart slightly and obscured his intelligence. You do not love war! Far from loving it, you gladly allow yourself to dream of a beautiful system of universal peace. Seat yourself on the throne, and it will not be impossible, your right hand armed with the scepter and the left with the ring, to realize your dream, to practice your system."

The second voice responds: "Mistrust the father of fraud, the prince of pride; it is him who is speaking to you! It is him who is circling you! It is not true that you need to be king in order to execute the beautiful conceptions of your loving and benevolent thought, since your influence is everything, as has just be admitted, since the king has no other will than yours. You could not act more directly, more immediately, in accordance with your wishes. Dispossessing Charlemagne would therefore have no other object than the satisfaction of a base covetousness; it would be an ignominious theft. Far be that vile fraud from you! Far be that cowardly pride!"

The first voice responds: "Even if I consent to suppose that your royal coronation would not be an absolute utility in the execution of your generous plans, it is not necessary for that reason to renounce it; for, on the other hand, there is an interest of a more sublime order that is even dearer to you, and without that coronation you can never make it prosper as much as you wish. Understand, then, that it would put you in a position to implant and consolidate forever the establishment of Christianity—which is to say that you, a priest, once solidly on the throne, could and should pass a law that perpetuates in the hands of priests the exercise of sovereign power, which forbids choosing successors to the throne other than from among them. Then, it would not be for yourself that you would be reigning; it would be to secure with you, and above all after you, the reign of the priesthood! The temporal domination of the Church is the indispensable complement to its spiritual domination.

"There is no true enlightenment except in the Church, is there? Outside of its bosom there is only darkness. Well, the property of light is to devour darkness. The mission of ecclesiastical order is to absorb secular disorder. Hence, in order to operate the salvation of humankind, it is urgent to unite human constraint with divine persuasion. Does one not read in the New Testament: *Compelle intrare?* which signifies: 'If you do not succeed in persuading consciences, force them by violence; save souls in spite of themselves.'[1] Now, is not the unique means for the ministers of Heaven to be able to exert that holy violence

---

1 The words are taken from *Luke* chapter 14, from a parable in which a master sends his servants to gather people for a feast; it was widely construed in Medieval Christendom as a licence for forced conversion, although it is difficult to believe that the words were intended to be construed in that fashion.

on terrestrial souls to constitute themselves, without division, the masters of the world? Seize the scepter, therefore, in order to lead the destinies of the Church sooner and more surely! Become king. *Ad majorem Dei gloriam!*"[1]

"Hypocrisy, infamous hypocrisy!" says the second voice. "Lies and impiety! In his Gospel, the Savior declares formally that his kingdom is not of this world, and he is careful to prescribe insistently respect for the rights of Caesar; and as nothing is contradictory in that sacred book, no word, no syllable, no true meaning authorizes priests to dominate temporally. It is only with the aid of the most damnable subtlety that one can extract the appearance of such a strange authorization. Oh, when one interprets the law of God falsely, it is because one wishes to do so, for everything there is formulated clearly, explicitly, with precision!"

"No! Everything there is not precise!" the first voice interrupts. "No, everything is not clear. Otherwise, what would be the use of so many scholars devoted to its interpretation? But that's enough, that's too much deliberation. It's time to make a decision, it's time to choose. Come on, rid yourself of these indecisive movements, this flux and reflux of hesitations, deadly clouds that will end up diminishing, and perhaps extinguishing, the torch of your reason and that of your will. Cease reflecting, commence acting. Plunge without reserve, entirely, into the glorious ends of your talisman."

"Yes," says the second voice, "that's right: don't deliberate any longer, make up your mind. Expel from your

---

1 "To the greater glory of God!" The Latin version is the motto of the Jesuits.

mind the examination of the pros and cons, the affirmatives and negatives. They are vapors and gusts from Hell, which might adulterate and even destroy the steel of your faith and the gold of your charity. Apply to yourself the wise words that you spoke to Charles one evening regarding the 'curious arts' and the prudent advice that you gave him regarding the Serpents' Egg."

It is thus that our worthy archbishop is floating, tempestuously, between the temptation from below and the admonition from on high.

Finally, he drops anchor . . .

He dominates his irresolution. He rallies to the advice that the two contrary voices have just suggested to him with a common accord. He decides; and he does so as a faithful Christian, as a loyal priest. He takes the dangerous ring from his finger and he throws it far into the lake, murmuring: "*Vade retro, Satanas!*"

The freshness of an ineffable tranquility glides through his veins and recompenses him for his pious sacrifice.

He begins to contemplate quietly the little lake, the beauty of which his tumultuous preoccupations had not yet allowed him to see. He is proud and happy to sense the calm of his soul in unison with the infinite calm of the water.

He is taking so much pleasure in that contemplation, and enjoying it so exclusively that he does not hear the footsteps of someone approaching him from behind. A hand falls on his shoulder with an amicable pressure. Charlemagne is beside him.

The king tries to speak, but the sudden aspect of the lake's magnificence dazzles him in his turn and stops the speech on his lips. He is fascinated. It is with great difficulty and great effort that he is finally able to put an end to the oppression of his ecstatic silence, in order to claim, religiously: "Oh, this lake is divine!"

There again, the inappreciable ring is having its effect.

Meanwhile dawn rises gradually between the fantastic slopes of the mountain chain by which the lake is partly surrounded on the horizon. Orange, violet and roseate tints are produced, mingling and confused amid the capricious wisps of ample vapor that undulate softly over the water. From that vaporous and luminous mixture, appearances and simulacra are born whose uncertain lines and vague floating curves deceive the imagination of those gazing at them. Charlemagne distinguishes therein, or thinks he can distinguish, the form of a pleated robe singularly impregnated with grace and majesty, in which a sort of feminine phantom seems to be moving, almost invisible by virtue of its ethereal transparency.

He indicates that to the archbishop with his finger, and says to him in a troubled tone: "That's like the radiant march of my Libania, isn't it?"

To which passionate remark the excellent Turpin refrained from refusing a sign of entire confirmation.

In conclusion, it was something durable and serious that suddenly infatuated the king with the beauties of that lake. He ended up contracting the habit of going to its banks regularly, every morning, stationing himself there for the greater part of the day, and even returning there sometimes by night.

He always took his friend the archbishop with him, and remained sitting for long hours, quite still, before that beautiful sheet of crystal and azure, absorbed in his vast amour for her—to such an extent that Monseigneur Turpin, eventually realizing that there was no means of curing him of that new bewitchment, said to him one evening:

"I share your special predilection for this place so much, my dear sire, that I dare to propose to you to edify here, not three tents, but a solid and complete castle for yourself, for the tomb of our Libania, and for me."

That proposition could not fail to please Charlemagne greatly. The next day, at dawn, a column on laborers laid the foundations of a new palace on the shores of the lake. The work was carried forward ardently. In less than a year, a royal edifice was constructed, which became Charles's preferred residence.

Inevitably, the seigneurs, curious to please him, hastened to build houses around it. From that agglomeration of manors soon resulted a majestic city that received the name of Aix-la-Chapelle.[1]

Thus, the palace and the city were the objects of all Charles's complaisance. Elected Emperor of the West, he established the seat of the empire there, and for the final and supreme favor, he wanted it to contain his tomb.

---

1 Nowadays known as Aachen and situated in Germany.

Epilogue

IT is a golden dream that sometimes consoles me
For the oblivion that awaits you, my frivolous dream,
The oblivion without awakening in which you will
    soon be.
It is on a summer evening, beneath the lovely Roman sky.
I perceive, in the Eden of a marble villa
A lady and her page sitting beneath a tree.
The page, by favor of the last fires of day
Has just read to his fay, to his lady of amour
This tale in which I speak of love and faerie.
Both of them, souls stirred and voices softened
With their assent lavish honor upon me.
There is so much indulgence in spheres of wellbeing!
When they have fêted well and blessed the poet,
An ecstasy grips them, luminous and mute,
In which the lady, over the proud lover's finger
While he kneels triumphantly, passes a charming ring.
Then, between them, a flame interposes: a mystery!
A flame that is best veiled, a mystery that must be silent,
As the gods are veiled and their grandeur is mute,

For the Muse and the priest have the same modesty.
Then the cloud descends, and the couple get up.

Respiring the balsamic sap of the great woods,
They walk at random along shady paths
Through the network of tenebrous thickets;
On the edge of the horizon the moon leans over
Watches and smiles at them like a Dame-Blanche.
Enlaced with one another they go lightly,
Like two seraphim which deign for a moment
To tread our humble soil, still sensing their wings.
Their eyes continually intersect their gleams.
Gladly, in her azure voice, the Marchesa
Hums a motif from Weber or Cimarosa . . .
Now she falls silent, happy to hear
The page, who recites this grave and tender sonnet:

I possess a ring whose gold, divine mirror
Absorbs my thought, my heart and my soul:
A fine talisman of sympathetic flame
Which I have from the amour of a dark-eyed fay.

I possess a ring whose chaste power
Renders ugly in my eyes any other than my lady
And makes her in her turn, for me alone, a woman
Whom my embraces alone can move.

I possess a ring whose holy faerie,
Of my dreams of amour and chivalry.
Has been able to realize all the ideal pride.

I possess a ring! If someone comes to steal it
When I am lying in the night of the coffin,
I shall resuscitate in order to reclaim it!

La Patrie, March-April 1842.

A PARTIAL LIST OF SNUGGLY BOOKS

G. ALBERT AURIER *Elsewhere and Other Stories*

LÉON BLOY *The Tarantulas' Parlor and Other Unkind Tales*

S. HENRY BERTHOUD *Misanthropic Tales*

JAMES CHAMPAGNE *Harlem Smoke*

FÉLICIEN CHAMPSAUR *The Latin Orgy*

FÉLICIEN CHAMPSAUR
The Emerald Princess and Other Decadent Fantasies

BRENDAN CONNELL *Clark*

BRENDAN CONNELL *Unofficial History of Pi Wei*

ADOLFO COUVE *When I Think of My Missing Head*

QUENTIN S. CRISP *Graves*

QUENTIN S. CRISP *Rule Dementia!*

LADY DILKE *The Outcast Spirit and Other Stories*

CATHERINE DOUSTEYSSIER-KHOZE *The Beauty of the Death Cap*

BERIT ELLINGSEN *Now We Can See the Moon*

BERIT ELLINGSEN *Vessel and Solsvart*

EDMOND AND JULES DE GONCOURT *Manette Salomon*

GUIDO GOZZANO *Alcina and Other Stories*

RHYS HUGHES *Cloud Farming in Wales*

J.-K. HUYSMANS *Knapsacks*

COLIN INSOLE *Valerie and Other Stories*

JUSTIN ISIS *Pleasant Tales II*

JUSTIN ISIS (editor) *Marked to Die: A Tribute to Mark Samuels*

JUSTIN ISIS AND DANIEL CORRICK (editors)
Drowning in Beauty: The Neo-Decadent Anthology

VICTOR JOLY *The Unknown Collaborator and Other Legendary Tales*

BERNARD LAZARE *The Mirror of Legends*

BERNARD LAZARE *The Torch-Bearers*

MAURICE LEVEL *The Shadow*

JEAN LORRAIN *Errant Vice*

JEAN LORRAIN *Masks in the Tapestry*

JEAN LORRAIN *Nightmares of an Ether-Drinker*

JEAN LORRAIN *The Soul-Drinker and Other Decadent Fantasies*